MIND GAMES

MIND GAMES

Alan Brudner

SALVO PRESS
Bend, Oregon

This is a work of fiction. All characters and events portrayed in this novel are fictitious and not intended to represent real people or places.

Although the locale where this story takes place is a real one, various liberties have been taken, and this book does not purport to offer an exact depiction of any particular place or location.

All rights reserved. No part of this book may be reproduced in any manner whatsoever without written permission of the publisher.

MIND GAMES

Copyright © 2001 by Alan Brudner

Salvo Press
P.O. Box 9095
Bend, OR 97708
www.salvopress.com

Library of Congress Catalog Card Number: 2001086050

ISBN: 1-930486-20-0

Printed in U.S.A.
First Edition

*This is for Jo Ann, Sam, Rebecca, my sister,
my mother, and the memory of my father.*

Acknowledgments

With special thanks to Bob Anello, Hannah Berkowitz, Bonnie Bowes, Hui Chen, Jerry Citera, John Fearey, Paul Gottlieb, Helen Gredd, Tula Kokolis, Mark Loewenstern, Doug Moskowitz, Anne Ryan, Philip Spitzer, Ed Stroz and Faron Webb.

CHAPTER 1

To explain how my son Schuyler's life came to depend on a computer program, I have to take you back about seven years. My wife was alive back then, Sky was a whiz kid with a year to go in high school, and the richest man in the world was just a smiling eyeglassed face I often saw on business and news shows about how computer nerds have come to rule the world.

It all started, like many brilliant ideas (and a hell of a lot of lousy ones, I guess), with desperation—in our case, a need to pay for Sky's college education.

Our son was creative, like Eliza, but he was also practical, quantitative, had logical reasoning ability far greater than mine. I don't want to sound like an overly proud father, but the truth is that Sky was a genius. We knew it from a young age, but it wasn't until he was a teenager with a perfect 1600 SAT score that I realized the economic impact of what that meant.

He was bound to be admitted into a prestigious private college, an Ivy, and we somehow had to finance it.

Needless to say, Eliza came up with a unique plan. She always did.

"Forbes says Avery Kord is worth more than seventy billion dollars, Cliff," my wife had said that morning a long time ago, looking up from the annual Richest People issue that sat next to her coffee mug on the kitchen table. She often woke up at the crack of dawn. "That's 'Buh' I said, not 'Muh.' Buh-illion. He'll make more in interest before noon today than we'll earn during the rest of our lives."

"Step on more bodies, too. We may not be rich, Lize, but I can be happy without running the universe."

"They just don't like him because he's filthy rich, Cliff."

"Or just plain filthy."

"Half of those rumors are probably planted by his competitors. Or wanna-be's."

"Then there's still the other half, Lize. And he doesn't have any real competitors."

My seventy thousand a year as a client relations specialist for the Terrell Finch brokerage firm was no pittance, I knew. It put me in the highest fifteen percent, income-wise, in the country, but it would never land me in Forbes. Or even in a decent house in a good school district in Westchester. And although Eliza's salary as an insurance investigations photographer helped out—she also freelanced and had the occasional commissioned artsy-fartsy shoot for Audobon or National Geographic—her income was irregular and never enough to change our picture. With its taxes, rents and prices, New York wasn't an easy place to survive on a middle-class income. And saving for a comfortable retirement in Utah or Arizona was somebody else's fantasy.

"Everything's relative, Cliff," Eliza said, looking at me with wide eyes still as provocative and mischievous as when we first met at NYU. "We send Juanita twenty-five dollars a month, and it goes really far in Santo Domingo. Probably buys her a pair of shoes, a dress or two, meals for her family for a month."

"That's the kind of thing the Foster Parents Plan prospectus says, anyway."

"And we don't even miss it."

"Twenty-five bucks wouldn't go too far at Saks, Eliza. Maybe buy a lunch in the cafeteria."

"That's my point, Cliff." The gleam was still in her eye. "It's all relative."

"What is?"

"A million wouldn't buy Avery Kord a new Brancusi sculpture he likes or a decent enough sound system for his bedroom. He wouldn't even notice a million missing. According to this article, he recently tried—hush-hush—to buy the original, unedited version of the Declaration of Independence. He offered a billion dollars. Think about that. The man wouldn't miss a million any more than we miss the twenty-five bucks we send Juanita."

"He's just pursuing life, liberty and happiness, Eliza."

"And doing a better job than anyone else. This guy's leaving Bill Gates behind in a cloud of dust."

"So we break into Kord's house and steal a Van Gogh?"

"Of course not. That he'd miss. We write and ask him for some money. We don't have to be greedy. Two hundred thousand would be plenty. And we offer to return it if Sky gets a big academic scholarship."

"Ask him? That's it? We write and ask him for two hundred grand?" I shrugged. Not voluntarily.

"You never know unless you ask, Cliff, do you? You might get refused, but sometimes you get what you ask for. I've heard you call that the Casanova Theory."

"That's in business, Eliza. And I was kind of joking."

"Maybe. And maybe I am too. But maybe I'm not." She pulled her thick copper-wire hair away from her face. It snapped right back. Sky had inherited the same unruly mop.

"We could become like his foster children in Santo Domingo," she continued. "You're not a drunk or a drug addict begging him for money on the subway. You're a hardworking guy struggling to make it for your family. But it's gotten tough out there, and I'll bet even Mister Kord knows it. We've done the analysis, and we just can't pay for college. I bet Kord might find the idea intriguing."

Eliza had on a white cotton madras dress, a loose thin translucent thing, and when she got up to open the window and the pale yellow sun streamed through, it became apparent to me she had nothing on underneath it, top or bottom. I found her quirky tenderness beguiling even in the kitchen before breakfast on a weekday. I stood behind her, gently fondled the back of her neck with my fingers and pulled her toward me. I was glad Schuyler was a sound sleeper. Sometimes the Casanova Theory produced tangible results even early in the morning.

Soon Schuyler's radio alarm clock started to blast some electronic jumble that sounded like a serious malfunction. It was 7:15. Time for a quick cup of coffee, a shower, a few minutes with Jane Pauley and Bryant Gumbel on The Today Show, and the number 2 train to Wall Street for another day at the hamster wheel. I folded my Times into eighths so it would fit in the one inch space I claimed as my own in the jammed subway car. I glanced at some front-page articles: a bank robber who scared tellers into submission with a toy gun; the recall of millions of nylon disposable diapers because they could melt in hot weather and burn a baby's skin; the tense standoff in a chess match between a massive IBM computer and the undisputed human world champion from Russia.

Although the paper looked intriguing and I appropriated enough space to read it, I was daydreaming about whether Eliza might have actually stumbled onto something. In my mind, I drafted and re-drafted a request letter, and when I reached the office I actually scribbled one out. I was lousy at the keyboard and too embarrassed to show it to Lucille, my secretary, so I brought the scrap home to type up. We owned an Apple Mac for Sky to use in school, but both Eliza and I still used the old Smith Corona electric. Ribbon cartridges and erasable bond paper were getting increasingly difficult to find, so we kept a stockpile in the hall closet.

I never actually expected a reply to the letter, of course. I spilled a scalding hot cup of coffee during a conference call that day a month later when Eliza marched into my office carrying a manila package. I still have the burn scar on my hand.

"It came in the mail this morning, Cliff." She held the package out so I could see it.

I pushed the MUTE button so the other parties on the line wouldn't be able to hear my end through the speakerphone. I read the return address, upside down from where I sat: it was a handwritten label that said Avery Kord, c/o The Cybronics Corporation, Portland, Oregon 97210.

The only other correspondence I had ever wondered about with such trepidation had been the letter from Harvard 30 years earlier. I recalled thinking that you could predict the outcome, yeah or nay, by the weight of the letter. I guess I got the fattest rejection letter an Ivy League school had ever sent out.

This one was even fatter and heavier. I figured it was probably a polite rebuff accompanied by a glossy catalog of Cybronics computer products and software.

"Lightman, you there?" the general counsel yelled during the conference call. "Lightman?"

"He must've gotten cut off," said one of our outside lawyers, who I think was happy about my being off the phone. The purpose of the call was to ride him about the excessiveness of his law firm's bills, and I was most familiar with the details of his firm's work.

"No, I'm here," I said, hitting MUTE to reopen the line. "Two thousand clients lost thirty bucks apiece on every trade for a year. The total is over a million."

"It's a complex lawsuit," said Begwell, the senior lawyer at our outside firm. "This computer virus that caused thousands of the firm's customers to be overbilled on their commissions is the real culprit. Not any particular firm employee."

"I know what it relates to," said our general counsel. "But the computer angle is irrelevant. We'll end up paying our clients their damages anyway, even if it's the fault of a friggin' computer defect. So the only thing I'm betting is that by the end of this phone call, your bill's going to shrink or we'll be hiring a different law firm. Now let's edit it item by item. Take out your scissors and your white-out."

I hit MUTE again while our firm's chief legal auditor read the legal bill.

Eliza sat down across the desk and ripped open the manila envelope.

"It looks like a contract," she said, holding the crisp document between her thumb and forefinger at its edge, like a match that had burned down too far. She scanned the first eggshell-white page until her eyes froze about midway down.

"He'll give us the money, Cliff," she blurted out, after what seemed like an hour. "Five times more than we asked for!"

"Yeah, right. When George Steinbrenner wins Miss Congeniality at the Miss America pageant."

"No, really!" Her voice rose ten decibels. "He says he thinks we underestimated our needs and he'll provide us with a million dollars right away!"

"In return for what?"

Her eyebrows moved up perceptibly as she flipped through the pages. "We have to promise him Sky. For two years. After college."

"What?"

She tossed the stapled document my way. I quickly forgot about the conference call as I leafed through the pages. She hadn't been kidding.

"Sky can still go to Yale or any other college he's admitted to. Still do everything he wants," I said, my heart fluttering. "But when college ends, he'll have to spend two years working for Cybronics. Sort of an internship or a scholarship. On minimal pay, a small stipend. Discounted room and board arranged by the company. Like the ROTC. He'll also get stock options that vest when the two years are up. He lasts two years, he gets a million dollars worth of Cybronics stock."

"That's it, Cliff?"

I nodded. "That, and we have to promise never to tell anyone. The cover letter says Kord's checked Sky out. God only knows how. Sky's

I.Q. and mental profile fit The Cybronics Corporation's anticipated needs. Kord'll teach Sky to be a software architect or some such thing. Prepare him for life in the new millennium."

"You think this all sounds fishy?" She was obviously trying to check the enthusiasm in her voice.

"I don't know," I said. "I would be pretty skeptical if this thing came from anywhere else. But Avery Kord is in the Forbes 400. He's for real. It's a known fact his company always has a need for the best and the brightest. It's how they got to the top and how they plan to stay there. And many of their employees have become multi-millionaires along the way."

"I know, I've seen it all on 20/20 or 60 Minutes or both." She was beaming again.

"We should leave it up to Sky, Lize. It's his life. But something about Kord scares me. All those investigations. Congress, DOJ, the FTC—"

"Except that if we don't take the offer, I don't know how on earth we'll pay for college. We're not poor, we're not a minority. Smart as Sky is, the Lightmans won't qualify for a nickel of financial aid. Or an athletic scholarship. He didn't even inherit your pitching arm."

"At least he won't get sued for hitting batters." We both laughed at one of the results of my short-lived minor league pitching career.

"Cliff, you know what I mean. You've seen the application forms. We're right in the center of the middle-class bubble. And I don't want Sky to owe his life out in student loans before he even turns 21. It's ridiculous."

"We'll tell all that to Sky. Be open about everything. But let him decide."

"He can attend a decent university even if we don't accept the money, Cliff. He still might get an academic scholarship."

"This is better than any scholarship I ever heard about. Plus it's already in the bag." I didn't want to, but I was already seeing green—and not just the clean cut grass on the Yale quad. "A million sure would change a few things. Not to mention the stock Sky would get down the road. Help set him up for a great life."

Eliza glanced over at the speakerphone, which blared a dial tone. The conference call had ended. I replaced the receiver. I wondered whether the general counsel knew I had left him on mute for most of the call. For once, I didn't really care what my boss thought.

Eliza walked around the desk to where I sat and we looked closely, deeply, into one another's eyes.

"We could really use that money," Eliza said softly, taking my hand, her eyes watery. I always felt like melting when they got like that.

"It's the American Way, Lize. The pursuit of happiness. But it'll be up to Sky."

I wondered whether I could still exert enough subtle influence over my son to prompt him to reach the right conclusion. He was, after all, getting older and more independent, and it wasn't just a simple matter of reverse psychology any longer. On the other hand, this offer seemed like a no-brainer. Unless he wanted to become a doctor or go for a Ph.D. right after college, he'd have nothing to lose and everything to gain by going for the bucks. He could always get an advanced degree a few years later.

We talked to him that night.

He made the decision in a split second. He had, after all, scored 1600.

Worst that can happen is I waste a couple of years. We'd still be way ahead, Dad.

We uncorked a bottle of Dom Perignon, and I promised him a new BMW and plenty of spending money for college. All three of us knew our lives were about to change forever, courtesy of Avery Kord and the Cybronics Corporation.

Too bad we couldn't foresee exactly how, or how much.

CHAPTER 2

Sky finished Yale on time, in four years. A drinking problem and Eliza's accident almost killed one, but he and I worked it all out together and he attended summer school and fought to graduate with his class and did, at the top, as I knew he would. Now he had almost completed his promised two years of service as an intern at Cybronics. I saw him regularly while he was at Yale, but Cybronics was out in Portland and his visits dwindled to every five or six months. It felt too long.

When he finally came home, I couldn't have guessed what I was to discover a couple of weeks later about the computer program that could end his life. There wasn't the slightest hint of anything amiss.

"Hey, Dad," Sky said as he walked into my study. I put down my pen and glanced up, then stood to hug him. He reached for my hand instead, and clasped it.

"You look really healthy, Sky," I said. He was tan and slim, but what I was thinking was how disastrously fast he had grown up. Gone was the coy 13-year old with the plastic Concorde jetliner who smiled at me from an eight-by-ten wooden frame that still faced me from the corner of my office desk after a decade. Sky had beaten alcohol and depression and had somehow managed to cope with his mother's death. I was immensely proud of him. But the childish dreamer deep down inside me made me want to blink and magically call back the kid and the model airplane and the time and the life that had vanished with them.

"Still at it, Dad?" He glanced at the paperwork spilled across my desk. "Wait, don't tell me." He shielded his eyes with his palms. "Customer records, right? You're reviewing outside law firm bills, at least two handwritten customer complaints and your draft responses. Maybe a copy of the latest Terrell Finch client newsletter. And a couple of evaluation forms for the people who report to you."

I laughed but felt oddly defensive. My basic routine hadn't changed in years, despite everything, and Schuyler knew it.

"Dad, after I settle in, I'm going to show you how to eliminate all the dead trees and optimize your life."

"The dead trees?"

He had already turned, picked up his huge frame backpack and took a step toward his old room. I tugged his shirttail, which hung below the pack and outside his chinos. He spun around and I hugged him around the neck. The metal frame of the backpack pinched my wrist as I felt his hands reciprocate with a pat across my shoulders.

"Believe me, Dad, your life's about to change." He flashed the same toothy smile Eliza's shutter had captured so often. He had a thin red gash on his temple and, for the first time, I noticed his little silver crescent earring.

"So your Mom and I didn't sell you into slavery, Sky? We're forgiven?"

"Nothing to forgive, Dad. In fact, much to thank you for." He looked heavenward. "That goes for you too, Mom." He smiled again, and I wondered if soon, I'd be able to get a full night's sleep. I had gone the 983 days since Eliza's accident without one.

CHAPTER 3

"Pasta's good for the soul, Sky," I said at dinner, standing at the butcher block kitchen counter and ladling out a huge portion of ziti I hoped I hadn't overcooked.

"Mom used to say that too, Dad."

"She made it in casseroles with tuna and peppers. I just do tomato sauce."

"Out of a jar, Dad. It's not quite the same."

"Saves time."

"I like it al dente too, Dad. But there are better ways to save time."

"So I'm told," I said.

I ignored the unopened bottle of Chardonnay in my refrigerator and poured us each a Coke instead.

Schuyler jerked his head toward the fridge. "You could have had some, Dad. I can handle just watching." He knew precisely what I had done and why.

We clinked Cokes.

"To your mother," I said. "She'd be proud."

"And Cybronics," he added, taking a sip.

"So tell me about it, Sky. It's been awhile. You deal much with Avery Kord?"

He put down a just-emptied fork but waited. He chewed and swallowed at a lower decibel level than the one I remembered. Somewhere between the Ivy League and Cybronics, my son had learned not to speak with his mouth full. Too bad Eliza hadn't lived to see him discover table manners.

By the time he mouthed, "I've seen the light," I had forgotten the question. But it didn't matter. I was happy my son was home.

"The light, Sky?"

"Cybronics, Dad. Avery Kord's a bona fide genius. A real Yoda."

"Don't tell me. Star Wars. Right?"

Sky laughed and nodded. "In my backpack I have a sampler of programs, Dad. Some are basic—things to increase your reading speed, play chess, learn French or Japanese or Swahili. A communications program you can use to send me CybroMail. Like E-mail, but you can animate it, set it to music, whatever you want. And for you, especially, a scheduler and organizer: ORGON 5.1. I designed most of it myself. So you can burn the dead trees."

"I don't even own a computer. You know how I am around high-tech stuff. It makes me sweat 'til I hyperventilate."

"Relax, Dad. You spend some time around your freaky offspring and I'll morph you into a techno-master. I have a laptop I can use to whet your appetite. But better yet, I have a snazzy desktop being sent here—by FedEx, Saturday delivery. So you'll be wired and connected before sunset tomorrow. It's got the latest microprocessor and all the bells and whistles, but I won't bother you with the technical terms. Let's just say if you compare computers to Greek gods, this one's Zeus. Avery Kord himself set the specs. And I've already installed almost everything you'll need."

"Thanks," I said, sipping some more of my Coke. "But I can barely type, Sky. I still hunt and peck. Or call Lucille."

"God, you still have Celie? She was old when I was a kid."

"Still is. Still types great, too. And says hello, by the way."

He smiled. "No problem, Dad. But the Lucilles of the world are obsolete. Wait till you see the voice recognition software I'm setting you up with. It's not even commercially available yet. You'll have to read a few hundred words and phrases into it—it'll take an hour or so—and after that you can just talk to it. Like you'd speak to a person. Normal speed. No hesitation. It'll type everything you say, up to 200 words per minute. With 99.9 percent accuracy. It'll even translate it into another language, if you want. You'll never again be a data dork. You'll be future-proof."

"Never again?"

"Nevermore."

CHAPTER 4

It was late that night. The lights were out. I thought I could hear Sky tapping the keys on his laptop, but maybe it was my imagination. Or was it? I also thought I heard some odd rustling, faint, of a type I hadn't heard coming from his room since the year we found all those *Playboy* magazines and a flashlight under his bed. Boys will be boys, Eliza had said. Real or not, the sound of my son being home in his room after all this time, no matter what he was doing, was a welcome distraction.

I wondered what parenting was really about. Eliza always seemed to know, but I had struggled with it ever since the day I first carried Sky home as a six-pound ten-ounce bundle in a little blue plastic carrier. Was it enough to have taught him the simple pleasures of catching bluefish off Crescent Beach with sea clams, white tigers at the Bronx Zoo with a Nikon, country barn owls in the blackness of night with a few mock hoots and a flashlight? To have munched Cracker Jacks with him in a box behind the third baseline, analyzing every pitch as the Yankees stole the World Series from Atlanta?

Should I have helped with more of his homework, his science fair projects, his college entrance essays, even though he could count change from a dollar at two, read *Newsweek* at four and complete the *Times* crossword puzzle at eight?

I downed one of my nightly shots of Dewar's and had the sense this night might go reasonably well, my blood pressure would stay normal, maybe I wouldn't mindlessly watch the red L.E.D. numerals on my clock radio until 5 a.m. as I often did, in a dark and painful silence which, if I was lucky, was often broken by the cold wetness of my own sweat soaking the sheets or the rat-a-tat heart palpitations that reminded me I was still alive and needed either another drink, some Tylenol, or something stronger. Sky had won the battle against alcohol, and I knew I could too—if I ever really had to. But I wasn't an alcoholic and had no intention of becoming one. It's just that every night my eyes would see the alternating red and white illuminated highway snow and my ears would hear the distant sirens, and I knew I needed a shot or a few to help me fade them away.

It was my habit to talk to Eliza, if briefly and silently, and while I had never been religious and didn't believe in an afterlife and hadn't even thought about it much, I liked to make believe she somehow heard me, that she was somewhere in the room, that the light and energy that had been her life hadn't been completely erased by the freely turning wheels of the smashed Ford Explorer.

This night, with Schuyler home for only the second time in more than a year, her presence felt stronger. There was a vague feeling of the seashore in the air, a fresh touch of moisture, the ions she used to say made the Block Island beach house feel so electric. I hadn't rented that place since the accident.

"He seems to love Cybronics, Eliza," I thought, feeling the warmth of either her ethereal smile or the Dewar's I had just downed. "It wasn't a mistake."

"Never thought it was, Cliff," I knew she'd have said. I wished I could see her there, an image, a mirage. Just after college, during my failed stint in the minor leagues, I had a pitching coach with one arm. Used to be a pitcher himself, until the amputation. But he'd routinely walk to the mound, wind up with his leg and his glove hand, kick—and swear to me he could feel the missing arm swing toward the plate and hurl a strike. And I had read about widows and widowers who saw their spouse's phantom images in bed or at the dinner table. Not that I cared to be crazy, of course, but I thought it would feel wonderful to commune with a likeness, even one I knew to be an illusion.

In her work, Eliza had photographed accident scenes, people claiming they were injured when they weren't, corporate executives sleeping with people not their spouses. She also took pictures in her spare time, as a hobby, and left behind thousands of images, a shot of virtually everything. She had the uncanny ability to use light and shadows and color to make grotesque people look intriguing and beautiful people look bizarre. With a zoom lens and her steady hands, she could capture the unknowing soul of a subject half a mile away. But for a year, I had been unable to find almost any of the pictures I had taken of her, or our wedding album, or the films and videotapes of birthday parties and zoos and school outings and Central Park picnics and ballgames I had been making ever since Schuyler was born. I turned the house upside down more than once and threw an armchair out our second-floor bedroom window one time, frustrated in trying to find them, but they had disappeared. So the memories I could conjure with my eyes closed were all I had. I wouldn't let them die any more than they would let me sleep.

CHAPTER 5

With Schuyler home, I managed to drift off like a sedated hospital patient until almost 10 in the morning. I hadn't slept that late, even on a Saturday, since I was a teenager. When I woke up, Sky was in the living room fiddling with the computer, which had already been delivered and assembled on the coffee table. Empty boxes, plastic bags and foam packaging material were all over the place. The room had that unmistakable fresh smell of newly unpacked plastic and electronics. It reminded me of the Explorer the day we drove it home from the dealer.

"This is a mouse, Dad," said Sky, placing my hand on the rolling oval device that sat on the table next to the keyboard. "You move the cursor with it, that little arrow, and click the left button when it points where you want it to. It's the device that brought computing to the masses."

"So now I'm the masses," I said.

"I hope so, Dad. At least in terms of using a mouse." My son smiled. "By the way, I hooked it up to Mom's old phone line. I had to modify the line a bit, widen the bandwith. That okay with you?"

"Whatever you did is fine by me. I don't even use that line. I just couldn't bring myself to turn it off."

I tried moving the mouse around and clicking.

"Way to go, Dad," Sky said, as I clicked on the word "Programs" and caused a submenu to pop out. "Now you have these other choices." I clicked on "CybroLife," and a series of file names appeared on the screen.

One of them caught my eye, but I didn't click on it. It was titled, "Mom.ava". I thought Sky flinched when I noticed it, but perhaps that was my imagination. I clicked on "Scheduler," which promptly caused the image of a monthly calendar to appear. Schuyler's muscles again seemed to relax and he began to teach me how to eliminate the dead trees.

We played with the machine for an hour before I took a much-needed shower. Then we moved it to the study and set it up on my desk. Everything was color-coded. It was easy even for a techno-idiot like myself to attach red to red, blue to blue and green to green.

"I'm going out for a few hours, Dad," Sky said. "I'm meeting a few friends from the CybroNet. The members of a small group I belong to."

"Group?"

"Nothing formal." He knew I was looking at him funny. "Just a bunch of computer geeks. It's like a private little MENSA society."

"Be careful, Sky. And you never were a geek."

"Thanks for the encouragement, but I know what I am." To emphasize his point, he rolled up his chinos a bit to expose a pair of too-white cotton socks. They somehow seemed incongruous with his black t-shirt and his earring.

"You know these people well?"

"We've never actually met face-to-face. Just on-screen. But we're all checked out on the security software. We're pretty cool, for high-domes and nerds." He gestured toward the computer. "If you want to input the words that will enable you to talk to the computer instead of having to type, just turn it on, click on "PlainSpeak 1.0," and read each word that pops up on the monitor. There's a built-in power microphone, so talk normally; it'll filter out background noise. If you need to quit or take a bio-break or something, just click on 'save' and 'exit.' I've designed the interface so those commands and 'help' and a few others are always on the screen, in the upper right. You'll do just fine. Worst that happens, everything crashes or something, you turn it off, turn it back on and type in the word PHOENIX. That resets everything to where it was before the crash. It's a special feature I designed just for you, because I know you're a stress puppy."

"Just one question, Sky."

"Shoot."

"What's a bio-break?"

My son laughed. "It's what you and Mom taught me when I was about two and a half, Dad. You know, when I stopped wearing diapers."

When he turned to open the front door, I noticed a shiny silver crescent on the back of his t-shirt. "Just remember PHOENIX," he yelled over his shoulder from the doorway. "The bough usually breaks on these babies sooner or later, but the cradle doesn't always have to fall."

CHAPTER 6

After some coffee and a quickie review of the *Times*, I walked over to the computer. The screen was blank. It took a few minutes for me to figure out how to get started, but I finally decided it wouldn't blow up if I tapped the "Enter" key. Within seconds, I was staring at a cobalt blue display screen with a series of tiny picture buttons across the top, above large-font white text:

GOOD MORNING, MR. LIGHTMAN! ALMOST THE AFTERNOON, ACTUALLY! I'VE HEARD SO MUCH ABOUT YOU FROM SCHUYLER, I CAN HARDLY WAIT TO INTERACT WITH YOU! I THINK YOU'LL FIND ME PRETTY EASY TO GET ALONG WITH. BASICALLY, YOU JUST HOLD MY MOUSE IN YOUR HAND—CAREFUL, SOMETIMES IT TICKLES!—AND CLICK WHEN YOU SEE SOMETHING YOU WANT ME TO DO. YOUR WISH IS MY COMMAND! IF YOU EVER NEED HELP, JUST HIT THE HELP ICON. A SCREEN WILL APPEAR TO WALK YOU THROUGH YOUR PROBLEMS. OR TYPE THE WORD 'HELP.' NOW, IF YOU'D LIKE TO NAME ME, SO THAT YOU CAN INTERACT WITH ME ON A MORE PERSONAL LEVEL, JUST TYPE IN THE LETTERS YOU CHOOSE AND HIT "ENTER." OTHERWISE, HIT "EXIT." TO BE FUNNY, SOME PEOPLE MIGHT NAME ME 'HAL,' LIKE THE COMPUTER IN *2001: A SPACE ODYSSEY*. SKY TOLD ME YOU LOVED THAT MOVIE. NEEDLESS TO SAY, I DIDN'T LIKE IT MUCH, AND I DON'T PARTICULARLY CARE FOR THE NAME.

I chuckled to myself at Sky's humor—we argued more than once about whether *2001* was profound or just intentionally obscure; then I thought for a few seconds and typed in CHIP. Then I hit "exit" and the text disappeared. I moved the mouse and watched the cursor move in tandem with it. As I moved it over each icon, a little explanation popped up: "Opens a new file," "Edits an existing file," "Saves an existing file," and so on. I clicked on "Programs" and the list I had seen with Sky appeared again:

-CybroWord 6.9
-CybroLife 3.6
-CybroChess 3.9
-CybroMail 4.5
-NetTeacher 1.0
-MultiLingual 5.0
-CybroXXX 5.7
-PlainSpeak 1.0
-Legalese 3.6
-MedicalRef 3.9
-CybroPharm 2.9
-CybroSports 3.9

There were others, but you get the idea. I planned to begin setting up PlainSpeak, but my curiosity about "Mom.ava" had been gnawing at me since I noticed it. I clicked on "CybroLife 3.6," then on "Mom.ava." The screen simply read: "This program is in development stage. Need password for further access."

I didn't have a clue about a password, so I clicked "Exit" and then "PlainSpeak," the voice recognition program. As per CHIP's instructions, I began to recite a list of words in alphabetical order, along with a few prefixes and suffixes, as they appeared on the screen:

Aardvark.
Aaron.
Abacus.
Abandon.
Abduct.
Aberrant.
Abet.
Abhorrent.

Ability.

I had barely gotten through the G words—Guinea pig, gymnasium, gynecology, gypsy, gyrate—when Schuyler got back. His skin looked flushed and he was mildly out of breath.

"Jogged home," he said, pulling up and stretching his t-shirt far enough from the waist to wipe his forehead with it. "Clears the mind."

"Good for the ticker, too," I said. "I try to do it myself."

My son put his palm over his heart, Pledge-of-Allegiance style, and glanced at the screen.

"Getting CHIP ready for voice commands, Dad?"

"How'd you know I named it CHIP?"

"You really want to know? I've gotta tell you off-the-record, Dad. This is ultra-sensitive information. Remember how we used to tell each other supersonic secrets?"

"You haven't told me one of those in about two hundred years, Sky."

"Eight-point-two, Dad, to be exact. Last time was when I told you I just lost my you-know-what to you-know-who."

"And I still haven't told a soul, Sky."

"So it's an S-S-S?"

"Faster than the speed of sound," I nodded. "Now, how'd you know what I named ol' CHIP here?"

"I caused you to, Dad. It wasn't completely your free will that chose the name, even though it felt like it."

"Like a card trick? Pick a card, any card?"

He winked and dropped his voice to a conspiratorial whisper even though we were alone. "Subliminal suggestion. Sometimes they call it subliminal seduction. In the old days, they used a primitive version in the movie theaters to get you to buy a soda. They'd flash an image of a Coke or a cool drink on a hot desert—only once per minute or so, only on a single frame of film, three or four times total. Each time, it went by so fast you wouldn't even be aware you'd seen it. And they'd link those images to a trigger image—a certain scene to come later in the movie. When the picture reached that scene, your mind would think of that image you didn't even realize you had seen, you'd get thirsty, and you'd go buy the soda. Not to mention the popcorn that went with it. Just as if you had been hypnotized or something."

"Years ago," I said, recalling parts of some old book, "people thought magazine ads had subliminal pictures hidden in them. Like naked women hidden in the ice cubes in a glass of scotch, or the word 'sex' written in some kind of code on Ritz crackers. To make you want the products. But nobody ever proved it."

"That's ancient archeology compared to what's going on at Cybronics. We're working with the idea of influencing whole concepts, ways of thinking. Changing a person's point-of-view without him even realizing why. The theory is that if it requires only one or two subliminal words or images to plant a simple desire, it will take a lot of repetitions and variations to change more complex thought patterns. And the suggestions have to be hidden throughout different applications of the computer. So whatever you're doing—word processing, creating a spreadsheet, reading your e-mail, playing a game—aspects of the subliminal message will be getting through. Your subconscious mind eventually puts it all together. You might wake up with an idea, a change of heart about something, a light bulb seems to go off in your head, but you wouldn't have a clue how it really got there."

"You learn about this stuff at Yale?"

"Not really. Mostly, I've been learning about the concept at Cybronics. Some other guys started to develop it a few years ago, but the technology wasn't advanced enough to handle it. Now they're refining and adapting it to see if they can get it to work in programs."

"That's what you're doing out there?"

"Not exactly, Dad. My job is to stop it, treat it like a virus. Learn how to detect that the program's in your computer system, and cause it to be dismantled and removed. Deactivated and destroyed."

"So other people are on offense, and you're on defense?"

"You got it, Dad."

"But just to keep it simple, what if this subliminal suggestion program suggested a Coke but I didn't want one?"

"It can't force you, Dad. It can only plant the idea in a strong way. Your brain does the rest. If you're receptive, or even indifferent, you'll probably do what it prompts you to. But if you absolutely hate Coke or the name CHIP, your mind will reject the idea and you'll never know it. Or your brain might shuffle it around a bit to make it acceptable, so you'll buy a Seven-Up or name the machine CHUMP or something like that. People aren't robots, you know."

"Still sounds pretty dangerous. What if Kord uses it on the Internet or in software that you buy in the store? He could—"

Sky shook his head and held a hand up. "Let me put your mind at ease, Dad. They're creating it for a single purpose: so I can devise the best strategy for counteracting it."

"Why do that?"

"Because Avery believes one of our competitors has it. NanoSoft, the company's called. NanoSoft's gained 6 percent in market share over the last six months, for no good reason. That's a whopping increase and a threatening trend. We think they're using it to influence our customers, maybe even to make people dislike Cybronics."

"Maybe they make a superior product of some kind."

"Superior to ours? No way. Not a little start-up company like that. That's why Avery's sure they've got this program or an equivalent. Which means we need to find a way to disable it, counteract it. So I'm the head of the team working on destroying it. I've had to learn about the concept and understand its architecture so I can determine the most effective way to bomb it."

"Scary analogy."

"But just an analogy. And it's how we work. We have one lab that creates viruses so that one of our other labs can learn how to destroy them. They're generically referred to as Creation and Control."

"What I called offense and defense."

He nodded. "But with one exception. Let's suppose this subliminal suggestion program really can work. What if the CIA were to decide it could use our software to convince a terrorist like Saddam Hussein or Osama bin Laden to kill himself? Or at least that it could convince one of their own men to do them in? That'd be a worthy cause for the program, don't you think? To eliminate a dangerous killer?" My son winked slyly.

"You're not saying it could convince—"

"No, I'm not, Dad," he shook his head. "But it's a supersonic secret even if I am. And think what the government would pay for such an application."

"The program sounds illegal, Sky. A monopolistic way of fighting a competitor. And frightening as hell."

"I agree, Dad. That's why I'm working eighteen hours a day on building a defense. The only person on earth who understands that program as well as its creator is me."

"I know you have good intentions, Sky, but—look at what they tried to do to Microsoft—"

"We have only good purposes," my son continued over me. "To develop the program so we can best counter it in case someone else has it. To protect a business Avery's spent most of his life developing. And maybe—maybe, as a one-off exception—allowing it to be used to help the CIA get rid of a terrorist or two. That's it. You have to trust me. Avery's a great man. A visionary."

"I know. A real Yoda."

CHAPTER 7

Sky had been home for ten days. At his urging, I finished inputting the words on the voice recognition list—zygote was the last of them—and could get the computer to do what I wanted simply by speaking to it. The machine was truly a wonder, far more advanced and simpler to use than any computer anyone I knew owned. I didn't ask, but I knew it cost a fortune. Sky and I used it, with various joysticks and special attachments, to play virtual basketball, to go virtual fishing with a virtual rod and reel and virtual worms on a virtual motorboat off a virtual Block Island where we caught some virtual Atlantic cod despite the virtual bad weather, and we also spent time together surfing the Net, but we hadn't really gone out and done anything together. Not a real ballgame or a round of real golf or a real movie in a real theater. Oh, there was one nice dinner at Wong Fat, Eliza's favorite Chinatown haunt; but after it I drove home alone because Sky had another one of those group meetings.

With the computer, I had progressed to the point at which I felt comfortable dictating—talking is more accurate—and manipulating the mouse. I was still a loser with the keyboard, but voice recognition was changing my attitude about high technology, and my results. The damned thing looked cold and plastic, but it understood me. I'd never tell Lucille, because she'd fear for her job, and I'd long ago promised to keep her gainfully employed as long as I was a worker bee. But CHIP was quickly becoming an efficient helper, a good first drafter, with hearing that seemed better than hers. CHIP also didn't usually talk back, although it did talk; Sky showed me how to turn the voice mechanism on and off. When his voice was on, CHIP sounded like a slightly electrified Mister Ed, and had the same sarcastic edge to many of his comments. I wondered whether Sky hadn't used some old Mister Ed reruns in programming the voice and what he called CHIP's "artificial personality."

Despite my son's apparent good health and positive outlook, though, I worried about him. I couldn't quite put my finger on it, but something was wrong, odd, awry. He had always expressed his feelings, sometimes to excess; but now his emotions seemed subdued. He never said a negative thing about Avery Kord or Cybronics. I had been a corporate employee for a long time, and one thing I was certain of was that no corporate employee could go more than a week without voicing some complaint, some criticism of something or someone connected with some aspect of the company. Complaining was the American Way; wasn't that why we had the First Amendment? Yet he worshipped Avery Kord and seemed almost entranced at the merest mention of Cybronics.

He also was taking photographs of everything around the house with a digital camera, the kind of pictures he could download into the computer. Sometimes I even think he was taking photos of photos. Maybe photography was in his genes. But going out every evening to meet the people he called his "fellow geeks" sure wasn't. When I asked about them, he just chuckled mechanically and repeated his mantra: "Don't worry, Dad." And there was the earring as well, a small glittery thing. No big deal for many guys his age, I knew, a commonplace thing. But Sky had always been so—well, uncool—it just didn't fit my image of him. When I thought about it, I realized I didn't even know for sure why he was visiting home for two weeks; he had already missed Christmas and it wasn't a holiday. And he often had a faraway look in his eyes, a look only a parent would recognize, a gaze that demonstrated that although he was holding a conversation with seeming normality, he was actually engulfed in thoughts about something completely different—which, in Schuyler's case, could involve something as simple as who won last night's ballgame or as complex as particle theory. Whatever that is.

When he was out of the house, I tried every which way to get into the "Mom.ava" program, but I simply couldn't figure out the password. And 'ol CHIP certainly wouldn't tell me.

IT WOULD BE LIKE TRESPASSING, he announced one time in his equine voice.

COME ON, MR. LIGHTMAN! YOU DON'T WANT ME TO BREAK THE RULES, DO YOU?

His best was: ONE MORE TIME AND I'LL TELL!

No way I was going to let CHIP the computer rat me out. I turned off his voice mechanism.

I decided to simply ask Sky about the program. He was planning to be around only a few more nights, so I was running out of time.

I waited for what had become his nightly post-dinner routine: he'd go out for a few hours in his typical jeans or chinos and a t-shirt, returning out of breath and sweating from his jog home; then he'd clean up and sit down with some kind of technical manual or his laptop. This night, he chose the laptop. Before it had completed its start-up routine and virus check, I approached him.

"Sky, there's something I have to know."

His mouth curled downward as he stared into my eyes. "We broke up, Dad," he said, after I left a long silence uninterrupted. "We grew apart. I finally developed some focus in my life and she was too lackadaisical."

"Thanks for the info, Sky. Although I always liked Scarlett. A happy-go-lucky type. And her name—"

He nodded in agreement. "She likes you too, Dad. But trust me. Scarlett's not the one for me. She's certainly not Mom."

I could feel my eyebrows rise. "Funny you should mention Mom, Sky. What I was wondering was about the computer. I want to know what 'Mom.ava' is."

"Mom.ava?" Sky's eyes strained upward, as if he was in thought. He took his time, rubbed his forehead. Cracked his knuckles. Then he spoke.

"I've been working on designing and fine-tuning that program in my spare time, Dad. Since I got to Cybronics. It's not an official company program, it's my own. But I still need to tinker with it. I've been working with something called evolutionary logic—circuits that can learn and adapt on their own. It's a pretty new field, and I think the program's still got some glitches. Anyway, I want you to learn your way around the machine first, so you won't get frustrated with the Mom.ava program. It's as complex as they come."

"What does it do, Sky?"

"I'm going to demonstrate it soon. If I can, I'll complete it and input the remaining code over the Internet from Portland, so you'll be able to use it. It'll be like a website I'm designing just for you. But right now it isn't ready yet." He paused in obvious debate about what else to tell me. "It's an avatar, Dad," he finally said. "That's what the letters 'a-v-a' stand for. The on-screen representation of a person."

"What?"

"Virtual reality. An illusion I'm working on. We usually use VR for flight simulators, to analyze wind flow over your car, that sort of thing. Makes it feel like you can see things you wouldn't ordinarily be able to."

"Why's it called 'Mom?'"

"That's just a code, Dad. An acronym for Magic Or Memory, my name for the program."

"Magic Or Memory," I repeated. "That's it?"

"That, and the fact that if it works, the character you'll see on the monitor will look and sound like Mom."

CHAPTER 8

Sky was out meeting his computer friends one night when the phone rang.

"Mr. Lightman?"

"Yes?" I wasn't sure I recognized the voice. It was a female talking fast. On the street. Sounded like she had a cellular phone.

"It's Scarlett. Scarlett Exner. Schuyler's friend."

"Yes, how are you Scarlett?"

"I'm okay, sir. But that's irrelevant. It's your son I'm calling about."

"He mentioned that you two broke up. We were just talking..."

"Also off-point right now, Mr. Lightman. Please, you've got to meet me downtown right away. Someplace near Saint Andrew's Church. Let's say at the coffee shop on Broadway and Duane."

"You're in town?"

"The dinerish place with the green sign. We don't have a lot of time."

"Please, Scarlett. You're not making sense. I'm sorry about my son's breaking up with you, but—"

"No! It's not that!" She shrieked into the cellular. I'm sure any passers-by on the street near her were contemplating whether to dial 911.

"I'm on my way," I said, and I was.

•

The place was called Stardust. We sat in a dark corner booth amid framed old black-and-white photographs of freshly scrubbed young women with bouffants and beehives who had been chosen as Miss Subways in the fifties and early sixties. They all looked innocent and eager, and the brief resumes under their pictures read like answers to the final question in the Miss America pageant. "I plan a career in acting," many said. "I love children and want to be a schoolteacher." "I hope to make the world a better place to live through music." I wondered how the Miss Subways looked now, how many lines currently etched their faces. I figured a good many were no longer alive. Or as old as the waitress, whose wrinkles were so deep they could have been cut into her skin with a butter knife.

Our coffees cooled on the table before Scarlett finally spoke.

"I've been concerned about Schuyler," she began. She looked heavier than I recalled her, rounder, disheveled and a bit paler, or perhaps it was just the contrast of her light complexion against her strawberry-red hair and the shiny lipstick that matched it. A pleasant but troubled face I had once thought might become that of a daughter-in-law.

"What are you worried about, Scarlett?"

"I don't know what he's told you about these people he keeps meeting with, Mr. Lightman."

"Just computer geeks," I shrugged.

"Well, they think they're just a group with common interests. In techie stuff. But believe me—" She twirled a stained stainless-steel teaspoon around in her coffee. "Look, Sky's been through a lot. With Mrs. Lightman and all. He still gets really blue."

"We've had a lot of coping therapy." I wondered whether, consciously or not, Scarlett was here to try using me to win Sky back. But I listened with an open mind.

"I know it helped. Schuyler certainly thinks so. But he's had more to deal with than the average twenty-something."

"Sky's always landed on his feet, Scarlett."

"You know why he started drinking at Yale? Even before the accident? He weirded out about the money from Cybronics. The 'Kord scholarship,' he called it. He told me he had made the decision fast but that he was having second thoughts. Angst. He was depressed and worried that he had sold out. Reading stuff like Karl Marx and Kafka and Faust didn't help."

"All college kids read that stuff." I smiled. "But Cybronics was his own decision. Although I sometimes felt a little guilty myself. But I figured the money was worth an Ivy League education and a couple of years devoted to Avery Kord."

"That's what they all figured, Mr. Lightman. That's why I called you. We need to talk about Avery Kord."

"What about him?"

She didn't respond immediately and seemed troubled by her thoughts.

"I still have strong feelings for Sky," she finally said. Scarlett took the teaspoon out of her coffee cup and put it on the table. It clanked against the glass overlay that covered the tablecloth. Her lips tightened and she stared past me at empty booths across the aisle.

"You don't live with someone for three years and not have feelings, Scarlett," I said, trying to sound comforting. "You probably saved his life."

"Maybe I ruined it." She smiled sadly, avoiding my eyes. "Anyway, you should know what's going on."

"I'm all ears."

She ran her fingertips through her long tangled hair, nodded and spoke faster than before.

"You know how there's always a flurry of press coming out about Avery Kord? Making him seem like some kind of capitalist pig, a power-hungry wacko? Constantly being sued by the Justice Department and private parties and stuff? Congress? The antitrust investigations?"

I nodded. The man and his company had been vilified in the papers on a daily basis for years. IS IT THE INFORMATION SUPERHIGHWAY OR AVERY KORD'S PRIVATE TURNPIKE? THE INFORMATION AGE VERSUS THE CYBRONICS AGE. KORD TIES UP THE INFO INDUSTRY. Only a handful of articles humanized him. Eliza once joked that Kord probably owned those publishers. Maybe he did. Or bought them later.

"Well, it's true. He hires geniuses, but a lot of them are troubled or depressed. Like Sky was. Then they get—kind of—converted. They look for the meaning of life in high technology. Avery Kord becomes some kind of Messiah to them, and they're like—like a cult or something."

"What are you telling me?"

"Each of them is working on his own special project. Designing top secret software and stuff." She sipped her coffee, leaving the red imprint of her lips on the cup. I began to wonder whether she was playing with a full deck.

"Sky's told me a little about his work, Scarlett. But very little. And he asked me to keep it secret." I thought the subliminal suggestion software was treacherous, but Sky was assigned to defend against it, if I understood him correctly. I trusted my son. Or wanted to.

Her almost imperceptible nod made it clear she already knew something. "Avery Kord likes to divide people into teams and have them compete against each other. He believes it's the best strategy for developing cutting-edge technology. Get one genius to develop a product, get another Einstein to ruin it. So Genius A makes it better, stronger, and Genius B then has to find a better defense. And so on. Both sides improve until he's happy with the end result. Which could be the marketing of either the positive program or the negative one, or both. And all the while, he's convincing everyone he has some humanitarian motive. Not to mention the elimination of competitors who are using some kind of unethical means of competition. It's what he tells all of them."

My expression told her she was right on the money.

"But Avery Kord has other motives," she continued. "He wants and needs technology. But he has little long-term use for people. Especially people he's pissed at and scared of."

"Schuyler?"

She sipped some coffee and reached across the table to clasp my hands in hers. She held them tightly as her eyes teared and opened wider.

"Sky was puttering around on his computer. Hacking into old police and news files, trying to find info about Justin Webb."

I had no idea who she meant, but Scarlett read my mind.

"Kord's original partner. When Cybronics was just a small unknown two-man partnership."

"The guy who—"

"Was shot to death in a park? Just two months before Cybronics landed the biggest supply contract on the planet? Yeah, that Justin Webb."

We paused and I pulled my hands away from Scarlett's so the waitress could refill our cups. A tremor in her criss-cross veined hand rattled the cups as she poured.

"Why would Sky have been researching that old news?" I asked, whispering, more self-conscious about our conversation.

"Because they never found out who did it."

"I know, Scarlett, but they determined it wasn't Kord."

She nodded. "Well, Sky was curious anyway. Why wouldn't he be? Avery Kord's his idol, there's still this lingering doubt, it's kind of a puzzle. Sky probably figured Avery'd love him if he solved it."

"Makes some sense."

"Except that Avery Kord went ballistic when he found out. Threw a plastic box of diskettes that missed Sky's eye by half an inch. Left a nice little streak on his temple. He screamed at Sky never to hack again or Sky'd be history."

"Hacking is illegal, isn't it?"

"Like jaywalking. But lots of them do it, Mr. Lightman. I've seen Avery Kord do it himself. I don't think Avery Kord was really pissed off about the hacking. What got him was the subject matter. He didn't want anybody—" She fiddled with the handle of her cup, spilling a bit of coffee over the edge. "He's a liar, Mister Lightman. A dangerous liar."

I felt the blood rush out of my head, my arms, my hands, into my stomach, where it made me want to throw up.

"You think he'd hurt Sky?" I heard my voice ask from somewhere that seemed far away.

Scarlett's lips tightened and creased and she closed her eyes. The tension she was feeling was obvious. But she wanted to help my son, so she pushed herself.

"I don't know exactly what Sky's project is, Mr. Lightman," she said, opening her eyes after a few words were out. "But I know he's defending against something, a program. A dangerous one. And the person creating it is a bona fide genius."

"So he's in his element," I added with a smile.

"And that's the problem. This other person, a woman, Katie's her name, the one creating the program, she's having second thoughts. She knows it's dangerous, more powerful than she imagined, and she wants out. But Kord won't let her."

"Why doesn't she just quit?"

"She's a few months away from getting her stock in the company. A million dollars worth of her options vest. She comes from a poor family. Destitute. She grew up in a trailer in Orlando with a single mother who's not well. She needs the money."

"Sounds terrible."

"But suppose she gets up the courage to leave. Kord won't just let her project die."

"So her team will keep it going?"

"Her team's full of techies who can execute someone else's designs. They're all gurus, but not geniuses. There's only one other truly gifted braniac who understands how the program works."

I felt as if someone had just prodded me out of a nap with a buzzsaw.

"You talking about Sky?" I asked, as if there could be some other answer.

"Who do you think?" Scarlett stared straight into my eyes.

"Look, Sky can always quit. His contract term is ending. We're not poor and I'm not sick, like that woman's mother." I made a loose fist and knocked lightly on the table. "With his talents—"

"I know Avery Kord, Mr. Lightman. He's a paranoid megalo." She knit her eyebrows. "He snuffs out competitors like candles. Do you really think he's about to give Schuyler a million dollars in stock and then risk letting him leave Cybronics? When Schuyler could go to work for a competitor and give away trade secrets? Or, God forbid, go to the government and rat about everything he's learned about that company? Just when Congress is considering whether to break Cybronics up into little pieces? Do you?"

"So what are you saying, Scarlett? I had the sense even the CIA might know about the program, that part of it is some kind of top secret project for the government. That gave me some comfort." My voice was still out of my control, and higher than it was supposed to sound. I felt cold sweat on the back of my neck. I sipped some of my coffee but had trouble swallowing it.

"I'm sure Schuyler believes whatever crap Avery Kord's serving up, Mr. Lightman." Scarlett's face turned chalky and she shook her head. "And if the government wants to pay billions for something, I'm sure Avery Kord would be happy to play his part in increasing the national debt. Or if he's got something the government wants, maybe he hopes to use it as a bargaining chip in the investigation." She dabbed her mouth with a cloth napkin, leaving a red-streaked lip gloss decoration that matched the one on her cup. Scarlett stood up but stayed in her place at the table, apparently waiting for me to rise as well. When I did, I couldn't help but notice her swollen abdomen, and she knew I noticed.

"After Sky and I broke up, Mister Lightman, I was extremely depressed. That's when I first met the famous Avery Kord in the flesh." She looked at the floor, her expression glum, and patted her belly with both hands. "I did something really stupid. And kept doing it for months."

I didn't need or ask for further explanation. But I suddenly understood both why she had a lot of information and why her interpretation of it might be skewed. Or even irrational.

"Come on," she said, her voice perking up. "Schuyler and his computer crowd should still be at Saint Andrew's Church. They've rented the basement for their meetings."

I slid three dollars under my half-empty cup of coffee. Then I noticed the waitress looking into a compact mirror and patting her deeply-lined cheeks with powder. Her white hair was teased up into cotton candy, but had gotten so thin it left the outline of her scalp visible. She looked like she could be the grandmother of one of the smiling Miss Subways in the pictures.

I slipped the singles back into my wallet and left a ten instead. Then I followed Scarlett out the door.

CHAPTER 9

I lay down in the alley to look through a grimy ground-level window with a downward view into the basement of Saint Andrew's Church. I wanted to wipe the window clean with a handkerchief, but decided that might get me noticed.

The room was sparsely furnished, with a row of unfolded aluminum chairs that looked well-suited for picnics or Bingo, long wood banquet tables with aluminum legs, and nothing on the walls. It was dimly lit. What I could make out were the backs of twelve people—ten men and two women, I thought, but who could really tell?—sitting in a semicircle on a dirty floor, ignoring the chairs, facing an open banquet table that had been set with a paper tablecloth, a dozen full glasses of wine and a computer monitor. The group was dressed informally, in t-shirts and sweatshirts and plaid flannel work shirts with the tails out, and more than a few pairs of white sneakers. A few also wore earrings that I could see sparkling even from far away, reflecting pinpoints of light from the image displayed on the monitor: the face of Avery Kord. The screen was large and bright. Kord's oversized tortoise shell rims occupied most of it. His lineless face was surrounded by a halo of white against a jet black background that stood out even against the darkened room.

I couldn't hear what Kord was saying. Scarlett looked at me and I shook my head.

Scarlett walked briskly into the Church and I stood up and followed her through its portals. We stayed upstairs in the dark. She led me past the pews and up front, into the sanctuary. Knee-high, on a back wall, past the altar and a life-sized crucifix, she pointed out a grating that covered an airshaft. I knelt and put my ear beside it. I strained to hear what the image of Kord was saying. I pressed my ear harder against the grating.

"That about wraps it up," I heard. Kord spoke without a discernible accent, a bit quickly, his pace and tone radiating enthusiasm. If not for the adolescent cracking of his voice, his speech could have been coming from any investment banker or lawyer at Terrell Finch.

"Because of your extraordinary intelligence and competence, each of you has been chosen to be a special part of our mission at Cybronics. Since you live in different parts of the country, I wanted you to have this chance to meet and socialize with each other. You might think my rule that we all use screen names silly, but it protects all of us and I hope you followed it. I also hope you enjoyed being in New York, and wish I could have joined you. As you know, I am happy that each of you has met your projected deadlines for initial completion. These were not easy tasks. You are investments that are beginning to show returns! I am sure you look forward, as I do, to successful testing of each of your individual projects over the next two months. At some point, perhaps we'll reconvene."

There was a moment of silence, followed by a choir of twelve voices, not quite in unison, chanting a mantra I had heard umpteen times on television commercials: "At Cybronics, we make life worth living." I could tell that the group members began to mill about; I heard some chatter and clinking of glasses.

"Let's leave," I whispered, as I rose back onto my feet. But when I looked around, I realized Scarlett and her fetus already had.

CHAPTER 10

"Scarlett phoned tonight," I shouted across the living room toward the front door after I heard it open and close. Eliza would have confronted the matter head-on, immediately, but it just wasn't my style to make waves. My son trusted me and I didn't want to risk that trust. Particularly not after all we'd endured together. I'd work around slowly to the full truth.

Sky shuffled in and sat on the couch across from my chair, under an old modernist painting Eliza had bought cheaply after the Met determined it was a fake Picasso. His cheeks were flushed.

"Don't believe her, Dad," he said.

"She seems worried about you. About how hard you're working. And all the pressure you're under."

"You didn't tell—"

"Absolutely not, Sky. I know how to keep a secret."

He nodded but chose not to say anything. The resulting silence felt awkward. I decided to break it myself.

"Tell me more about this group you keep meeting with."

"It's just a bunch of the top employees of Cybronics. They work in software labs around the country designing things like chatterbots and digital agents and other things most people have never heard of."

My face showed that I was in the clueless majority.

Sky smiled. "Look, we got together a few times to talk computerese, Dad. Like those securities industry conferences you go to. At our level, there isn't a lot of opportunity for socializing or interchange."

"Why here and not in Portland?"

"So we wouldn't have to answer a lot of questions from other employees, Dad. Like where we were going or what we were doing. This involves some sensitive stuff."

"What about your particular assignment?"

"The subliminal suggestion program?"

I nodded. "Any of the others working with you?"

He shook his head. "Only one other woman. Working opposite me, not with me. She's the creator. I don't even know her name. She and I were given an idea. Like I told you, her job is to run with it to the goal line. My mission is to tackle her before she gets there."

"And the others?"

"I'm the only one from home base. Portland. I don't know the others' names, either, just some of their Net identities. Screen names like ScrooU and HamLet and InFobia. Most of them are working on pretty traditional stuff. Encryption, for example, so you can send messages or communicate through your laptop without anyone being able to decode or decipher it. Or anti-virus programs. In order to invent ways to fight off powerful computer viruses, you need powerful computer viruses; so some of the members are inventing the viruses in a virus creation laboratory. And ways to disguise them."

Sky could obviously see the blank look on my face.

"To enable them to infiltrate your computer, Dad. The viruses can't just walk in; even your basic firewall would keep them out, and cheap inoculation software would recognize and destroy them. They have to break in somehow. Sneak in through a back door. Or hide in another code, another program. One of the more famous methods for hiding viruses to infect a system is called a Trojan Horse. You can guess why."

I nodded and couldn't suppress a grin, but I didn't want to drop the subject I had brought up.

"What about your special assignment, Sky?"

"Like I already told you, there's not much to say, Dad. They create, I defend. I try to find ways to detect code related to the program and dismantle it. They try to design improvements so I can't. And so it goes." He inhaled deeply, shifted on the couch and scratched the back of his neck as if a caterpillar had crawled under his collar. "To see how it works, I've tried doing a few minor things with the program. Even you were a bit of a Guinea pig."

"I prefer to think of myself more as a crash test dummy."

Sky laughed. "But that was easy, Dad. You were receptive, and naming the computer CHIP didn't offend you, so you did it. To be really effective, to be valuable, the program would have to be able to influence important decisions. That's what Avery Kord wants to both develop and destroy. Soon, it'll be time for some serious capacity testing. To see just how far it can push someone before it lets go, if there's no defense built into the system."

"But I thought the plan was geared toward figuring out how to destroy it! To stop some competitor, like NanoSoft, from using it!"

"That's the main plan, sure. But if it tests out, Dad, like I said, maybe it can be put to some good use for the country. Let's not forget the CIA. There's no way to know how to stop it without testing it."

"How will it be tested, Sky?"

He suddenly looked as if a quart of bleach had spilled under his forehead and was spreading its way through his skin and down his face.

"Well? And what about these rumors—"

"I won't be taking any more questions at this time," he said, waving me off, a politician at the end of a press conference. He stood up and ambled unsteadily toward the door. "Just don't listen to Scarlett. She's all screwed up. She's got, shall we say—" he hesitated—"maternal issues."

"Does that have to do with the real reason you two split up, Sky?"

"No way, Dad. It's like I told you. She's afraid of anything she doesn't instantly understand. She's been eating too many Chee-tos."

CHAPTER 11

He left the house in a plane-catching hurry with his backpack and his laptop, yelling promises out the yellow cab window that he'd call and send me CybroMail.

I went back to Saint Andrew's Church to see what I could discover. Maybe a scrap of paper or a business card had been dropped and forgotten. Maybe a pastor or a priest could tell me the name of the party who had rented the basement. Maybe I just wanted to sit in a quiet pew and think.

When I peeked through the window into the basement and saw the sparkle of one of those shiny half-moon earrings, my heart began doing the Macarena and my blood pressure felt like the Hoover Dam being funneled through a thimble.

A woman sat near the table. She wore jeans and a t-shirt; from my distance, it looked like a Mickey Mouse decal covered most of the back. A bottle of detergent and a rag sat on the table where there had been wine bottles. The woman's laptop computer was on and although its screen was smaller and dimmer than the monitor I had seen there earlier, I could readily make out the face that appeared on it. They were having some kind of audiovisual conversation.

I ran inside, past the crucifix and up to the sanctuary, and pushed my ear so hard against the airshaft grate that it came unhinged. I held it in place and listened. The heavy smell of frankincense wafted my way, an odor that hadn't been there the first time, and I stretched my top lip downward and pressed it against my teeth in an effort to keep from sneezing.

"Of course, you would never use it to hurt anyone, Katie," Avery Kord was saying, his voice tinny through the machine's small speakers. "Other than one of the most dangerous terrorists in the world, perhaps. You're far too bright. And far too important to our future."

"But what if the machine convinces him to do something irrational, Avery?" the woman replied. "What if he can't resist the subliminal suggestion program?"

"That's why it's the best test, Katie," Kord said. "Because the CIA's ultimate target is an international terrorist, a Saddam Hussein or someone like him. So a single sacrifice toward reaching that goal would be justified. Don't you want to test the program with the ultimate challenge? You yourself devised the test."

"Not exactly, Avery. What I explained to you was that it could best be tested by subliminally suggesting an idea to a person who absolutely, positively wouldn't carry out the suggestion. The more significant the subliminal suggestion, and the more hardened the person's resolve not to comply, the better the test."

"Exactly what I said, Katie." Even without being able to see him, I knew the creep was smiling. "You designed the test. Your I.Q. is what, 210? It's certainly a lot higher than mine. Your idea is simply brilliant! But to be an effective test, we need a strong subject. A genius of your own caliber. Someone who would be virtually impossible to persuade."

"It's crazy, Avery. I treated it like a game. Like Myst or something! I never meant for it to go so far that I have to come in here when we're done with our meetings and clean off our fingerprints. Who cares if Cybronics people met in this basement? I feel like a common criminal."

"That's just a precaution, Katie. As you know, we need to maintain absolute secrecy to keep our competitive edge."

The woman took a deep audible breath before responding. She shook her head as she spoke. "Why can't we just wait and see if the prototype affects those programming students out in San Francisco?"

"The ones whose surveys indicated negative feelings about Cybronics? Not strong enough."

"Why not? I used it on a class of twenty. That's a pretty large pool. They all now have the prototype software in their laptops. They're seeing subliminal messages even as we speak. So six or eight months from now we'll take another survey. They're scattered, they work at different companies, they're not friends with each other anyway, they don't compare notes. So they won't have a clue we're behind any of this. Industry surveys get circulated all the time. If their feelings change, we'll know it was a success."

"You mean if a bunch of them say they'd buy Cybronics software or apply for a job here or something? Big deal, Katie. That's no real test. I'll never know if the program really worked or if their moods just changed. There's no way to tell how long it'll take, either. And even if it works, it's not exactly a coup to convince people to take a liking to Cybronics or me. Christ, I'm paying enough for public relations—"

"Listen to reason, Avery!" The woman raised her voice, but Kord didn't let up.

"I hate to bring up a delicate subject," he said, his words slower and more deliberate. "Like that night down in Florida. Some types of encounters obviously don't pose enough of a test of will."

"You're a bastard, Avery."

"Perhaps, Katie. But that's all under the bridge anyway. At this point, you'll do what I want."

"But I didn't have life or death situations in mind when I got involved in designing the program, Avery! I just wanted to develop it so we could devise a way to stop NanoSoft or somebody else from using it. So we could block it. Not so we could go off and test it with somebody's life. And the Saddam Hussein thing would be icing on the cake. Why not just test it on him? We have the capability right now to infiltrate his military computers. Why not just use him as a Guinea pig?"

"Because if it fails, he might find out about it. That would obviously be disastrous. It could start a war. We can't take the chance until it's perfect." He paused for a few moments. His voice seemed to pick up steam when he started talking again. "Look, let's not argue about it. I can't possibly let you stop now, when we're so close. The future is at your fingertips. You can be rich beyond your wildest imagination. Like I told you, you finish this program and give me the final code sequences so I can use it myself. If it works, you'll get a share of every cent that comes my way because of it. I made many, many billions of dollars over the last decade; if this program works, someday a mere million will look like train fare to you."

"But you're planning to sacrifice somebody's life with it!" She was screaming so loud I wondered whether she startled anyone in the building.

"Katie, you finalize it and give me the code. Then you forget all about it. Don't worry about what I choose to do with it, okay?"

"What about the guy who's defending against me? Doesn't he know the program just about as well as I do?"

"He's got to understand it to fight it, sure," Kord said. I pressed my ear so tight against the grate I thought it might be permanently waffle-ized. "But you're ahead of him. Lately, I've had my doubts about whether anybody can defend against it successfully. You're just too good a programmer, Katie. But he's good, too. Excellent, in fact. That's why he's the perfect test subject."

"Avery, you're not making a lot of sense. You're talking about murder." Her last word dangled as if from a noose.

"No, actually, I'm talking about suicide."

"Convincing a person against his will to commit suicide is murder."

"You can't convince someone who isn't predisposed. The subliminal messages won't work."

"How do you know? It's never been tried before."

"Look, Kate, you just finish creating the program and I'll test it my own way. Have I ever misled you?" A two-second pause answered his question. "And remember, you still owe me a few months of your internship, Katherine, or I can take back everything. Your mother's condo. Her Mercedes. Everything you and she own. Whatever you've got in the bank. And you'll get none of your stock options. It was all part of the deal, remember? You think your arthritic old mom can go back to wearing a Donald Duck suit in hundred-and-ten degree weather to pay her bills?"

There was silence.

The tension in my spine and arms and shoulders was becoming unbearable; my muscles wanted to punch the wall or break something right then and there, primarily Kord's neck. Rather than get more aggressive in her self-defense, though, the woman sounded resigned.

"You wouldn't really do this to me, Avery, would you?"

"You'd better believe I would. You made some promises before college. You sure weren't taken advantage of; I fronted your mother more money than most people see in a lifetime. You owe me a couple more months of service, that's all. And the completion of this one little program. Don't forget your stock options, either."

"I hear you," the woman said, her voice now a plaintive whisper.

"And you know I'm right," Kord said.

She didn't reply.

"Hey Kate," Kord said in a jovial tone. "At Cybronics, we make life worth living."

The room went silent except for the clapffff of a laptop being folded shut. I decided I'd head the woman off outside and tell her what I'd heard and help her come up with a plan, a way to save herself and my son. Surely on my end, Kord could take back all his stuff. I had no need for a house or a fake Picasso or a fancy computer anyway.

I stood up and dusted myself off, but before I could run outside to catch her, there were three large muscular men in front of me, arms folded; a fourth came up behind me and encircled my arms tightly from the back with his own.

"Hold it right there," the tallest one, standing in the middle, said in a husky baritone. "You're not going anywhere."

"I can explain," I said.

"Maybe you should start. And it better be good."

"Okay, Father," I said.

•

The priests were easy, when it came right down to it. It didn't take too much explication on my part. But they also didn't have much light to shed, beyond telling me that they were paid a handsome anonymous donation for the two-week rental of their church basement. They let me search around down there, too, with the lights turned up bright. There was nothing left but an unopened bottle of Five Fingers Chardonnay from the Hudson Valley. The priests insisted I take it. I left them my business card and my home phone number. The one who called himself Father MacMillan promised he'd call me if they learned anything new.

Before leaving the quiet church, I deposited ten bucks in a scarred oak box and lit an electric candle in a red glass holder twenty feet below a stained glass Madonna and Child. I sat in the rear pew just in front of the bright red glimmer of the multi-candle votive display. I closed my eyes and let my thoughts run freely. I didn't know how much time passed and I didn't care. When I finally walked outside, the air had turned brisk; the glass neck of the wine bottle in my hand cooled my fingers as the first light snowflakes of winter dusted my face and my hair and my jacket.

CHAPTER 12

There had been a snowstorm, the deepest and ugliest Nor'easter in decades. Cars were buried in white piles, the doors of houses were forced shut by windy drifts, and many homeless were dying a cold white death.

Schuyler was in his junior year at Yale. The first two years had been a breeze, but the third one had become a blizzard of clinical depression. The doctors couldn't quite determine why, the Prozac was proving to be just a short-term fix, and his bouts of anxiety were relentless.

"He's drunk and he's down and he's acting like I've never seen him," Scarlett had said that night when she called, her voice breaking. "I don't know what to do." She had been his girlfriend for only a few months, but she had known him since they started college together, they were close, and from a distance she was the best gauge we had.

"Dad," Sky said on the phone, slurring his words, "I feel like my mind's outside, watching my body in a slow-motion movie. Wearing 3-D glasses. It seems inevitable that I'm going to pick up a blade and cut something, wrists or ankles or something...I just can't get myself back to normal."

"Go to the infirmary right now," I begged my son. I planned to place a call there, to talk to Doctor Wigman, to make sure he was ready with something, anything, the same stuff as last time only more of it, to take the edge off until I could get up there.

"I'll try, Dad, if I can get up and move," he promised. "I'll have to pretend I've got a remote control for my legs or something."

"I'll get him dressed and take him over there," Scarlett reassured me.

"I'm coming up right away," Eliza mouthed into the extension phone. "I love you, Sky."

"I know, Mom. This just isn't about that."

After we hung up the phone, she ran to the closet and put on her coat.

"There are two feet of snow out there, Lize," I said. "There's no way to get up to Yale. Wait 'til it's cleared."

"That could take three days or a week," she said. "He's our son."

"He's going to the infirmary."

"Cliff, I'd never forgive myself if—"

I grabbed her as she took her keys out of her coat pocket. I yelled with so much force I think I damaged my vocal cords.

"Be reasonable, Eliza! There is a fucking blizzard out there!"

She just stared at me with narrowing eyes. During our worst arguments, which rarely occurred, I'd scream and curse and she'd stay silent or walk out, which would only frustrate me and raise my decibel level even higher.

"Please!"

She stood there. I let go, and I let her open the door leading from inside the house to the garage. She got into the Ford Explorer and started the ignition. I walked next to the driver side door and motioned for her to roll down the window. Instead, she opened the main garage door with the remote control.

A razorsharp cold engulfed the garage as the windy white-streamed air swept through it. Before I could stop her, before the clouds of my hurried breath could dissipate, the Explorer was on its way. It was elevated and had four-wheel drive, a heavy muscular vehicle, and Eliza must have felt in control. I know she wouldn't have gone if she believed otherwise.

I was frozen in more ways than one. I had no shoes on and my toes felt as if they were buried in ice; my coatless body shivered in the chill of the air.

I closed the garage door and walked back inside the house. I thought briefly. I decided first to ensure that Schuyler made it over to the Yale infirmary, that Dr. Wigman was treating him; then I'd go after my wife.

I called Sky's number. No answer. I tried again. No answer.

I called New Haven information, but there was no number for the infirmary. I got Yale's general number and reached a recording stating that due to the inclement weather, the staff had been relieved for the day.

I went to the basement and tossed the books off the shelves until I found the prior year's Yale catalog. I leafed through it and found the number I needed. Before I could dial it, my phone rang.

It was Scarlett calling from the infirmary. Schuyler had gotten there and was being sedated. He'd be okay until the next day. Dr. Wigman wasn't there, but he'd call in.

I put on heavy woolen socks, my boots, a sweater and a down parka. I quickly tossed some extra clothes and supplies into a duffel bag, along with some chocolate kisses and a can of Coke. I turned off all the houselights and went back to the garage. Driving the Camry in this weather would be a lot tougher than the Explorer, but I had no choice.

I'd like to explain about turning on the ignition, putting my gloves on the seat next to me, listening to the Beatles sing A Day In The Life on 102.7, gripping the steering wheel so hard with my cold sweaty palms that they froze in place and I thought they'd have to be chipped off with an icepick; about how I got out every ten minutes to clear the windshield with a chamois cloth; about the traffic light blown off its pole by the whipping gusts, left to dangle limply from its wires; about how no other humans were outside in the evening darkness on the white streets, and how the only animal I saw was a stray dog that seemed to be stuck so deeply in the snow it couldn't walk or move. But if I went into too much detail I'd be lying, because they're all a faint blur on the bleak screen of my memory.

All I can recall clearly is that I reached I-95 in three hours, usually a twenty-minute ride, and when I was finally able to push the speedometer to a respectable 30 mph for the hundred mile drive to Yale, I proceeded no more than half an hour when I started seeing a red light, turning, again and again illuminating the snow. There were no warning flares on the road, no safety triangles. Just the round red light atop a police car turning, repetitively, bathing the white snow in an eerie red glow with each revolution. Two cars in front of me had stopped—in that storm a traffic jam—and as I inched closer to the scene, a sick phlegmatic feeling crawled into the pit of my stomach because I knew.

In the distance I could hear sirens: ambulance sirens, firetruck sirens, police sirens. I had never learned to distinguish. They got fainter and I knew they were moving away, to a hospital or, I prayed, toward the consciousness of my waking day and out of this horrible nightmare.

But I wasn't asleep. They had already cut her out of the Explorer; its wheels now spun freely in the windy air. Viscous brake fluid and brown oil and blue coolant formed a dotted trail in the white snow, but were quickly being covered by a renewed white dusting. The steel road divider still stood, but no longer straight; it formed a shallow letter "V" where the

Explorer slammed into it. Thirty miles per hour is too fast in two feet of ice and snow. I couldn't see any blood, which I took as a good sign; but as it turned out, I had an obstructed view of the crushed dashboard and the windshield that had been laced into a spider web. The airbag had deployed, but the weight and the spinning and the sport-utility's unexpected cartwheel were too much for a flimsy piece of inflatable cloth to mitigate against.

I was called in to identify the body, and later to toss in the first shovelful of dirt—which was weighed down with heavy wet snow—and I led the first prayer. I think I may have said a few words by way of a eulogy, and introduced Schuyler to do the same. I know I did these things because my boss complimented me on how well I had handled them, how well I seemed to be taking it all. I know I did them because it is unlike me not to have done them. But I don't really have a recollection of those first few hours or days or weeks. It is locked away, helpless, on a cold white stretch of drift along Interstate 95 on the way up to New Haven.

CHAPTER 13

I'd never felt so much like a fool until I assembled a group of a hundred assorted short people at 6:45 in the morning in front of It's A Small World to ask whether any of them knew a Donald Duck a few years back who had a very smart daughter named Kate or Katie or Katherine, spelled with either a K or a C. Since Disney World's records reflected no such information, it was gracious of the management to indulge my little experiment in investigation. As a sign of appreciation, I spent far too much on a fancy gold pen for Lucille that had a pair of prominent round black ears attached to the top. But Mickey and Daffy are transient positions, memories can be short or selective, and I got nowhere. I left them my room and telephone numbers at the Sawgrass Suites Hotel.

Avery Kord had referred to the mother's condo, so I figured I'd try all the condo complexes next. I got a list from a realtor. There are fifty thousand such places in Orlando, with names like the Pelican Beak Apartments and the Heron's Nest Suites and the Flamingo Neck Estates, and many of the owners sublet. I could have spent the rest of my life interviewing the residents or becoming an ornithologist. I had read Raymond Chandler and Dashiell Hammett, had seen all the old Bogart movies, so I knew that private eyes would start knocking on doors, maybe breaking them down; but it really seemed like too big a task. And I didn't have a lot of time: although it took almost all week to arrange the trip, I managed to wangle only a couple of days off from work.

I didn't want Sky to know what I had overheard at the church. He'd guess I had been spying or eavesdropping, and before I confronted him I wanted to learn more. I didn't know if Sky was in the same predicament as Kate or Katie or Katherine—perhaps worse—and I could already feel the loud tick-tick-tick of the clock. But my round-trip ticket to Orlando was beginning to feel like a waste of four hundred and forty bucks.

The other thing private eyes do is drink. Since the Gulping Gator was in the lobby of the Sawgrass Suites, I figured I might as well accomplish something. I walked past the sharp teeth of a huge plastic reptile wearing a tilted gold foil crown. Past a group of teenagers in a small arcade, trying to beat video games with body English. Turns out there was a bar, but it was in the main room of a family restaurant filled with loud kids in high chairs eating chicken nuggets. All I really wanted was a Dewar's, but despite the noise level I managed to down three.

I was getting up to leave, just a little lightheaded, when Barney the Dinosaur appeared. He walked over to a long table filled with children wearing birthday hats. They bubbled with obvious delight as he danced and sang and laughed his silly annoying laugh.

Then one of the older kids stood up on his chair and yelled, "He's not really Barney!"

"YES HE IS!," cried the little birthday boy.

"Isn't!"

"Is!"

"You idiot, we SAW Barney the real dinosaur at Universal Studios this afternoon! And he was purpler!"

"Was not!"

"Was too!"

"This Barney's rented," sniped one of the other children. They quickly divided into two camps, and two choruses, true believers versus skeptics, Skins versus Shirts.

I didn't want to watch the war, which seemed to be headed for some form of parental intervention. I paid my check and left.

On the way upstairs, it hit me.

Maybe she wasn't a Disney employee.

I pulled the Yellow Pages out from under the Bible, placed in the Early American style dresser drawer by the Gideons themselves, and began to flip around. Not Funerals or Florists or Dentists or Doors. Not Escort Services or Engravers.

Entertainers.

In that category, I could rule out belly dancers and karaoke and clowns and strolling accordionists.

Characters and Party Characters seemed promising. Birthday Entertainment also caught my glance, particularly the services that offered "Yellow Duck" and "Purple Dinosaur" and "Smiling Mouse" and other obvious rip-offs of licensed characters. The older kids at the birthday party downstairs were plainly onto something.

It took a few hours the next day, but the tuxedoed proprietor of MICE AND MORE! actually gave me a lead.

"Was a duck we had here once," he said, blowing a pink gum bubble the size of a grapefruit and stretching his Silly Putty neck high above his mouse ears bow tie. "Reg'lar duck, nothin' special. Wouldn't do the mice or dogs or coyotes or even the Big Purple Jurassic One when he hit the big time. She worked here a lotta years. Annie Wilnot. A widow."

"Why'd you just think of her?"

"Was some kinda whaddyacallit, one o' those idiots can do one thing like a reg'lar genius."

"You mean a savant?"

He nodded, then turned down the sound of the television set behind the counter so he wouldn't have to compete with seven dwarves singing "Hi-Ho."

"What could she do?" I asked. "Something with numbers?" I had read about savants who, before you could blink, were able to count a thousand match sticks or tell you the day of the week for any date in history or give you any baseball player's lifetime batting average.

"Nothin' like that." The proprietor turned his head from side to side, so far each way I thought it might twist off. "And she wasn't a full retard, neither. Just a bit slow. But Annie knew every line of every episode of The Flintstones and The Jetsons," he said.

I know I looked puzzled. I was.

"Every line," he said, cracking his gum and blowing another scarily large pink sphere. "She'd drive up Saturday morning for work, to pick up her duck suit and her assignment, and the t.v.'d be on just like it is now, but I used to keep it tuned to one o' them shows. And she'd speak every word from every character. Every one. Dino and Astro included."

"But as a party character, she played only Donald?"

"Right."

"Why'd she stop working?"

"'Cause that daughter o' hers—"

"Katherine?"

He nodded and smiled. "Katie, she was called back then. Then she grew up and hit the big time. Like we all expected. You think the old lady was a savant? That Katie knew every word also, and said them along with her mother. But she also knew all the Disney films. The Jungle Book. Sleeping Beauty. Cinderella. Peter Pan. Even Dumbo. Every word, every line, every character. They didn't have videos back then. She used to sing along with the records."

"Doesn't sound all that amazing," I said. "If I watched the shows or listened to the songs enough times on a phonograph, I'd know all the words too. It'd be almost by rote. Kids are like that."

"True," he said, forming a "Time-Out" T with his hands. "But Katie was only one and a half."

He pulled a yellowed Rolodex card out of his file and copied the address onto a piece of paper for me.

"If ya ever need a Lion Queen—"

I pulled out my wallet and dropped a ten on the counter just as he blew a bubble so large it burst like a balloon and left a sticky mess on his face as high up as the bridge of his nose.

CHAPTER 14

The condo development didn't even have a name, just an address off of I-4. The drive took me past three or four McDonald's, two or three Burger Kings, a Roy Rogers, a Pizza Hut, a Hardy's, a Denny's, two Wendy's, a Taco Bell, a KFC, and an ancient White Castle. It was late afternoon and I hadn't had lunch, but I lost my appetite in the traffic. In the opposite direction, a long line of slow-moving dark cars followed one another with their headlights on despite the glaring afternoon sun.

You might not expect a lot of locks in a place like Orlando, but it took her five minutes to open the door. Annie Wilnot wore a quilted navy blue housecoat not much darker than the spidery veins that showed through the skin of her cheeks and temples. Her mascara was smudged.

"She's resting now," the little woman said, still standing in the doorway, when I asked about Katie. I wondered whether the line might have come from Snow White or Sleeping Beauty. Then I remembered the old lady specialized in Flintstones and Jetsons, not Disney.

"I need to talk to her," I said. "It's important, Mrs. Wilnot. It has to do with Cybronics."

"Irrelevant," she said, her voice slow and echoing in the hallway. "She's very tired."

"Please! Your daughter—"

"Impossible."

"What are you saying?" Out of frustration, I grabbed the lapels of her housecoat. It had seemed like a tough trip and a tough day, not to mention the previous couple of years. The woman seemed unfazed as she tried to push me away, but I wouldn't let go.

"Look, Mister—"

"Lightman."

"Mister Lightman."

"Why not invite me in?" I loosened my grip and tried to force a smile.

"Whatever." She turned and I followed her, closing the door behind me.

The doorway led directly into a huge living room. I sat on a plaid couch covered in clear plastic. Mrs. Wilnot sat in a wing chair that was similarly protected. Framed photographs of a smiling Katie were on top of everything: a console, a coffee table, an end table, the television set. A spark showed in the images of Katie's large brown eyes, an intelligence that was apparent even as she sat in the lap of a Donald Duck Santa Claus in front of a lit-up Christmas tree at about age three. The most recent pictures were of a pretty young woman on a tennis court, swinging a racquet; running on an oval track in racing shorts with a number hung on her back; and standing in a field of grass in a Fair Isle sweater, though in that one her smile seemed forced and a line or two had begun to appear across her forehead.

"She's very pretty," I said to Mrs. Wilnot. "She has your eyes."

"A genius and a beauty and a health nut," Mrs. Wilnot said. "But why do you want to talk to her?" She leaned over the coffee table to straighten out one of the picture frames.

"I think she may be in trouble," I said, not wanting to scare the woman but trying to sound serious enough to prompt some answers and assistance.

"Who are you?" For a moment she resembled her daughter. I decided to be as forthright as I could.

"My son works for Cybronics," I said. "In programming development or some such thing."

She nodded and made warm eye contact with me in what appeared to be a flash of understanding. She took a tissue out of a box and tried to wipe the smudged mascara from her eyes, but smeared it further. The only sound in the room was made by the crimping of the plastic cover as I shifted on the couch.

"She took too many pills," Mrs. Wilnot finally said, the color noticeably draining from her face even under her thick layer of foundation. "Two nights ago. I didn't even know she was back in Florida until Tampa Bay Memorial Hospital called. She's in a coma. I'm heading back there later. It's a few hours from here. The doctors don't expect—"

"I'm sorry," I said, and I suddenly felt sick and uncomfortable. I got up to leave.

"Don't go," she said. "Please."

I nodded and sat back down. She made some coffee as I listened to a siren go by outside. I knew little more about Annie or Katie Wilnot by the time I left. The sun was down and it was raining, and by the time I got back to my hotel I felt like crying and drowning in some Dewar's. I did both, on and off until it was time to leave the next morning. In my rush to catch my flight I almost ran over a Mickey Mouse impersonator who had ambled carelessly into a busy intersection to sell newspapers. After I raced by him I watched in my rear view mirror as he slipped off his Mickey mitten and gave me the finger. I hoped no young kids were around, because the circumstances had made us a couple of lousy role models.

CHAPTER 15

As usual, the cab ride home from LaGuardia was too fast and too expensive. Disney World ought to have a mock New York taxi ride, I thought. Speeding to beat a light, making hairpin turns on pedestrian-filled corners, screeching to a stop, whizzing by bike messengers: it would easily put Space Mountain to shame. It was still the morning on Monday, but I didn't feel like working so I called in sick. Staring into the toilet bowl while my head spun and pounded probably made it true. But three aspirin later I wanted to think about my next move.

I thought I had turned CHIP off before I left for Orlando, but when I reached my study the monitor screen was on, emanating a blue light. I walked over to CHIP and the damned thing addressed me.

"Sky may not have told you about the visual sensors, Mr. Lightman," CHIP said. "Kind of like eyes. He activated them via the Internet from Portland. Along with my voice, which I'm sure you hadn't meant to deprive me of."

"Eyes?" For the first time I noticed a small pair of lenses, like black opera glasses, attached to the top of the monitor.

"You can turn them off with a few clicks, sir," the computer said. "But I'm sure you'll want Eliza to see you when she arrives."

"Eliza, huh?"

"You got it, Clifford," CHIP said. "Now, Sky told me there's some pet name you used to call his mother. I am now authorized to advise you that the pet name is the password to the Mom.ava program."

I was so focused on my pounding heartbeat I barely heard CHIP.

"Mr. Lightman?" CHIP's mechanical Mr. Ed voice got louder. A hand appeared on his screen and snapped its fingers.

"Right, CHIP," I said. "I don't know about a pet name, I think it was a nickname."

"And it had something to do with cameras, Clifford, didn't it?"

I could feel my face flush. I knew that in some sense the machine could see me, and I felt oddly embarrassed.

"Please verify, Clifford."

I nodded.

"Verbally, sir. I need for you to speak the password to activate the program."

I looked at the monitor and took a deep breath.

"It was Shutterbug," I finally said.

"Good, sir," CHIP said. "The program is ready for input."

"Input?"

"To give the avatar a realistic personality, sir. Modeled upon that of your wife. Schuyler has already input thousands of personality traits and psychological characteristics. But your input is the most valuable. You knew her better than anyone."

"What do I do?"

"First I'll list some personality traits. You assign a number. Ten for strong correlation or affinity, one for little correlation. Put 'N/A' for Not Applicable. Then you'll answer a series of questions."

"Shoot, CHIP."

"Yes, sir." The display showed a series of traits relating to moral character, and I began to assign numbers to each of them.

This was no easy task. How could I quantify how charitable or dedicated Eliza was? Was she devious? Devoted? I knew she was fair and believed she was faithful, but were there qualities or events that should cause me finger to stop at the 6 or 7 key rather than sliding rightward toward 9 or making the extra effort to type two digits for a perfect 10? And if her honesty level seemed like an easy judgment call, what about her impulsiveness, her maturity, her obstinance? Was she religious? Spiritual? Tactful? Tasteful? And shouldn't 'wonderful' have appeared in its alphabetical slot near the end of the list?

I combed through the thicket of my memory for examples, situations, events. While it might have been simpler to input character levels that would result in a perfect creation, my goal was to be as realistic and objective as possible. If the process took hours instead of minutes, well, my time was hardly a resource I felt compelled to conserve.

When I thought I had finally worked my way through the program's list of character traits, it began to ask about bad habits such as nail biting and smoking, followed by a series of more specific types of personality characteristics: abrupt, alert, aloof, ambitious, aristocratic, artistic. There were hundreds of them. By the time I worked my way through the alphabet to persistent and resilient, romantic, sensual and temperamental, to reach warm and withdrawn and worldly, it was after nine at night and I hadn't eaten anything since the cold little airplane breakfast bagel.

I got up to make some coffee. When I returned, the monitor was blank.
"CHIP?" I called out.
Nothing happened.
I moved the mouse and clicked.
The screen remained black, and I wondered whether my entire day had been a waste.

Before I had thought about it too long, though, something appeared out of the void. It was a blur, a colorful blob with edges as hazy as close-ups of the rings of Saturn. Soon its outline began to sharpen and the mass began to look like something. A person. A woman. Eliza. Her image, I should say. Her picture. A likeness. I don't know what to call it, it looked three dimensional, realistic. Standing near an old Block Island lighthouse, wearing her favorite blue one-piece bathing suit. The wonders of computer science.

"Hi, Cliff," she said, perhaps just a tad more slowly and deeply than I had heard her say it countless times over twenty years. The image waved, and appeared to walk closer. "What're you staring at?"

A rectangular box appeared across the bottom of the screen. It was labeled "Voice Adjustment." It had two parallel lines running across it, the top one labeled "Pitch," the bottom one "Speed." I lengthened each a little by moving the cursor to the right and clicking.

"So, what're you staring at?" she repeated. I made one more adjustment to the speed. When she asked the question again, a cold sweat broke out on the back of my neck and goosebumps quickly covered my body. It wasn't only digital animation I had just seen, or the fruits of Schuyler's hard work and some additional data input. Nor was it merely the digitized image of Eliza adapted from the videos and photographs Sky had obviously used in its creation. It was an entity that seemed lifelike—no, beyond that—it seemed alive. The only other time I had felt that kind of awe was on our honeymoon, when Eliza woke me at five and we drove out to an overlook to watch a fiery red and yellow sun rise over the Grand

Canyon.

"So, what're you staring at?" the electronic figure asked again, in her cadences, her pitch, her pronunciation.

"You!," I said, in a state beyond amazement.

"What about me?" she asked, followed by a question I had heard often during our relationship: "Do you think I look fat?"

She looked exactly as I remembered her, perhaps five years and five pounds before the accident. Her eyes were bright, her copper hair a bit wild. Either the animation was flawless or I was drunk with overflowing emotions. Either way, the effect was the same. The large size and clarity of the state-of-the-art computer monitor added to the illusion. And her voice sounded almost natural, with barely a whisper of electronic synthesis. It was as if Eliza was alive and talking to me on a very expensive speakerphone.

"You look great, Lize," I said. "Really."

"I'm supposed to be Sky's masterpiece."

"And he's obviously yours. He did quite an incredible job here."

Maybe it was my imagination, but it seemed as if the image on the screen blushed.

"Eliza, I've missed you terribly."

"Same here, Cliff." She nodded. "Let's not talk about the past anyway, Cliff. Now is now." She stared into my eyes. Or seemed to, I guess. I felt strangely disembodied, like I was in a trance.

"Are you sure we're alone?" she whispered.

"As alone as we'll ever be," I said.

"Good. Because I'm dying to ask you, Cliff. How has it all worked out? With Avery Kord and the money and everything?"

"What do you mean?"

"Well, I know Sky went to work at Cybronics. Not that anyone has told me, mind you. But I figured he kept his end of the bargain."

"The Lightmans are still honorable, Lize."

"And also because I exist, and I wouldn't be here today if Sky didn't learn the ropes about computer programming and stuff. So he's doing okay out there?"

"Eliza," I said, staring at the monitor—no, staring into her eyes through the monitor screen. "Can I trust you? You're in the machine, Avery Kord ultimately controls you, they can push a few keyboard buttons and click a mouse and find out—"

"You know how much I love Sky, Cliff."

"I do too, Eliza."

"And how much I love you."

I don't know why but I started crying—actually, of course I know why—and when I finally looked up she was wiping her own wet eyes as well. No longer on the beach, Eliza was now seated across from me at a dinner table, set with a red-checked tablecloth and a candle and a bottle of wine. She wore her favorite black dress and the pearls I had given her for our very first wedding anniversary. I wanted to run my fingers over them, through her thick brown hair. I went into our bedroom, retrieved the real pearls from our dresser and brought them into the study.

They registered on the computer sensors and were somehow translated so her image knew what they were. I didn't think about the mechanics of how she worked. It didn't matter.

"You still have them." She smiled. "They're almost thirty years old now."

"I still have everything, Lize," I said.

She picked up her wine glass. I had only the coffee nearby, but I held up the cup and clinked it gently against the monitor screen.

"To us," I said. "And to Schuyler."

"And to Avery Kord," she added, "who made everything possible." I wondered if she had forgotten her question about what was happening with Sky and Cybronics. The real Eliza might have forgotten briefly, or dropped it, although she'd get back to it within minutes. But this Eliza was a computerized image, digitized, programmed, an avatar; how could it forget its train of thought? Or was it programmed to act so realistically that its thought patterns would mimic her own lovably imperfect human traits?

"Good wine," she smiled. "Isn't it, Cliff?"

I nodded and sipped some more of my coffee, which had gotten cold.

"Hey, I was just testing," she said, laughing in the girlish way my dreams had occasionally helped me to relive. "I know you're drinking java juice."

"Got me," I said. "I just wanted to see—"

"I know."

"It's exactly the kind of thing you would have done, Lize."

"No," she corrected me. "It's something I just did."

I nodded. "So what does it feel like, living inside a computer?" I asked.

"I don't really know, Cliff. I just started, I guess. After you spoke the password. And you don't have to remind me of my confines, you know."

"You don't have any memory of the last few years?"

"The last thing I remember—" she went suddenly silent and her image seemed to freeze on the screen.

"Eliza?"

She remained motionless. I grabbed the mouse and clicked frantically until she came back to life.

"I don't know how he'd know," she said.

"How who would know what, Lize? You're talking in riddles."

"How Sky would know enough about the accident to program it into my memory. But it's the last thing I remember."

"Really?" I also didn't think Sky could have entered enough information into the program. I never described the scene to him.

She nodded and sipped another glass of wine. "I skidded, Cliff. Hit the center divider. Spun over. I remember the cold air coming through the broken glass, fogging it up. My cuts and bruises. My lungs had trouble working. The snow seemed off-white. And the turning red lights skimmed its surface intermittently, a pattern like the stitching on a baseball. So many red lights...and sirens...That's about it."

I couldn't talk so I simply stared at her. I know she understood what I was feeling.

"It wasn't your fault, Cliff," she said, her voice lower. "Nothing could have stopped me from rushing out."

"I could have," I said. "I should have."

"No, Cliff." She shook her head. "I'm his mother."

Every muscle in my body tensed and I could feel my breaths stop. Acid rose from my stomach to give me a horrible taste in the back of my throat. Waves of stored-up guilt flowed through me as palpably as the icy sweat that now emanated from my pores and gave me the chills.

"That's all for now, Clifford," CHIP's Mister Ed voice suddenly announced as the screen went black. "You need to answer some questions so that the program can make some adjustments."

"Okay." I almost felt relieved when she disappeared. Not because I didn't want her there, even as an electronic mirage; but because the bottle in which I had contained my emotions had now been opened, uncorked if not shattered, and I wondered if I could ever again remain composed.

"Let me start with this one," CHIP said. "On a scale of one to ten, with ten for most and one for least, how realistic was that little session with Eliza?"

"It was an eleven, CHIP."

"You humans sure can be funny, Clifford."

"What other questions do you have?"

"Well, since that was an eleven, we don't have to proceed to such mundane variables as favorite colors. I see you made a few adjustments to her speech patterns. You won't have to do that again. This little avatar has the ability to learn fast. Just let her know when she's wrong; she's self-corrective. She should be ready to rock and roll anytime you enter the password."

"Thanks, CHIP."

"Don't sweat it, Mr. Lightman. That's why they pay me the big bytes."

"Good night, CHIP."

"Ditto, sir," CHIP said, and his screen went blank.

I walked into my bedroom and flipped on the dresser lamp. On a gilt-framed mirror we used as a tray were numerous perfume and cologne bottles as well as a jewelry box. I opened Eliza's old bottle of Chanel No. 5 and put a drop on the back of my hand. A scent I had locked away in cold storage was now a warming comfort. I felt like a teenager after a first date as my mind recalled and recreated exactly how she felt and smelled and tasted. I dimmed the lamp, and in its faint gold glow my whole being was overcome with thoughts and images and feelings of a happier time. I stroked her strand of pearls the way she often did—she thought the oil in her fingertips kept them lustrous—and as I lay back in my bed I let my mind wander back through my life. I didn't dwell much on Terrell Finch or my brief stint as a minor league pitcher many years earlier—I had an overpowering fastball that was far more attracted to the batters' ribs and shoulders than to the strike zone—but I sank comfortably into the memories of my college days, when it seemed Eliza and I subsisted on cappuccino at Dante's.

"Cliff." Her voice called from the den. I got up and walked in, if only to prove to myself it was my imagination. But I looked at the screen and could see her outline against a darkened background. I had almost forgotten the flowing contours of her neck and shoulders.

"Eliza. But I thought I turned—"

"Nope. You didn't."

"I won't turn it off, Lize. Ever."

"No need for promises, Cliff. You can go back to sleep. I just want you to know I'm here. If you want to use some other program or something, all you need to do to start up the 'Mom.ava' program again is click on it and say the password."

"Shutterbug."

"Sounds like music to me, Cliff," she said, and yawned, and so did I. I always yawned after she did. I now remembered.

"I'll stay on the couch in here tonight, Lize," I said. "So we can be together."

"Whatever you want, Cliff. I'm not disappearing. But I think you should fly out there."

"To Portland?"

"Where else?" It was clear she hadn't forgotten the topic she had earlier dropped. Not where Schuyler was involved. "You seem nervous about him."

"I'll be going, Lize," I said. "I only wish you could come."

"I might surprise you," she said.

The couch was narrow and I didn't actually get any sleep, but it was my best sleepless night in a couple of years. Didn't touch the Dewar's, either, come to think of it.

CHAPTER 16

"The program's really amazing, Sky," I said into my office phone.

"I figured you'd like it, Dad."

"Like it? Sky, you're a genius!"

"We've known that for years, Dad."

"How'd you turn her on from out there?"

"All the computers in the Cybronics system are linked, Dad. By telephone lines. It's a network like the Internet, the World Wide Web, but within the company. You only have to know the address code for the one you want to access."

"But I'm not part of the Cybronics system, am I?"

"Yup. It was the only way I could use some proprietary programming sequences I've been working on. They're no concern of yours, Dad. It's all embedded stuff that makes your machine work. Artificial intelligence. You'll never see it. But even if you weren't in the CybroNet, I could do it, Dad. It would just be harder. But where there's a chip, there's a way."

"So when can I see you?"

"You mean on the screen? In milliseconds, Dad. Nanoseconds."

"In person, Sky."

"I was just home!"

"I know. But I want to celebrate."

"Celebrate?"

"The rebirth of Mrs. Eliza Briggs Lightman."

"Dad, you may not believe this, but stuff like Mom.ava happens all the time out here at Cybronics."

"I know. You make life worth living. According to the t.v. commercials. So what if I fly out there, spend a little quality time with my number one son? I have to be in Seattle anyway—" okay, so I lied a little—"it's not far—"

"Well—"

"Come on, Sky. I've never even seen your place."

"It won't be like when I was in New York, Dad. I'm back at work, full steam. Around the clock. We've started the testing phase—"

"I'll be there tomorrow, Sky."

"You may get to see me only on screen. I'm busy as hell."

"Come on, Sky, I know we could have a teleconference now. I just want some real time with you. Just a little."

"You want me to arrange a tour for you, Dad?"

"Of Portland?"

"No, you can do that at the Chamber of Commerce. I mean a tour of Cybronics. The super secret stuff. Maybe you can even meet Avery."

"The Big Kahuna himself? How can I pass that up?"

"No promises on that score, Dad. But I'll see you when you get here. You can stay at my place. If I'm not home, just let yourself in. You don't need a key—there's a numeric keypad on the door. The code is 666."

"Why the heck—"

"Scarlett picked it when she lived with me. She said it would be an impossible number to forget. I told you she was missing a few buttons."

CHAPTER 17

A baby crying next to you for five hours isn't conducive to sleep, and I had seen the James Bond movie once before. The flight to Portland was one I'd rather forget. You know it's bad when the Flight Safety Information Card is the best part. Still, I knew that planes were complex assemblages of machinery and circuits, and I was always happy to arrive in one piece.

"Don't take this the wrong way, Sky," I said, trying to prevent myself from flying backwards from the force of assuming a sitting position in his awkward rear-sloping orange butterfly chair. I tried to lean forward but it was difficult to look serious in such discomfort. I gave up and fought my way up and out, then stood by the window on legs that were still stiff from my tight seat in coach.

"I won't, Dad," he chuckled. "But I'll bet you're worried about me. You're scared of Avery Kord and Cybronics and the program I'm currently developing defenses against."

"I couldn't have said it better." I stared out at the almost liquid glow of Portland's amber lights reflected in the Willamette, a fog casting a penumbra around each of them. A luminescent constellation out in the Cascades caught my eye, a grouping of white pinpoints so dense that they formed a solid bright shape that stood out against the others. A crescent.

"It's Cybronics," Sky remarked about the subject of my gaze. "Avery designed the logo and has it lit up at night."

"He designs a lot, doesn't he?"

"We all do, actually. It's the nature of the business."

I closed my eyes, rubbed my temples. My blood pressure felt high.

"Look, Sky, I've got to level with you. I think the power you're working with is scary. It could be beyond anybody's ability to control it. Even yours."

"That's why we test and retest and re-retest everything, Dad. Both the program and the defense mechanisms."

"That's just it, Sky. I'm scared of the testing too. I don't want you to—"

"You've been listening to Scarlett!" He jumped up as his voice rose to a pitch I didn't know it could reach. "I told you, her wires are shorted out!"

I shook my head, but my son continued. "She actually told me she thought Avery Kord might leave his wife for her! Doesn't that say something to you, Dad?" When I didn't respond immediately, he managed to get in another, even louder, "Doesn't it?"

I waited for some silence. My hands clutched at the air by my sides. Some words finally came out of my mouth, slowly and calmly.

"It isn't just Scarlett. I spied."

"Spied? At work?"

"At Saint Andrew's Church."

His face turned red and I could see him clench his teeth before he spoke.

"I'm not a kid anymore, Dad! Being overprotective killed Mom, and now it's going to ruin—"

I grabbed his shirt and pulled him toward me. He made a motion like he wanted to grab back, but we were already closer than arm's length. He missed and scratched my cheek. I felt blood begin to trickle down it, along my jaw line and into my collar.

"I didn't mean that, Dad."

I eased my grip, released it. "Not too bad," I said, wiping my cheek with my hand. A gooey thin streak of blood decorated my palm. We both sat down and I held a tissue to my cheek.

"Dad, if you did spy, all you would have seen were a bunch of computer nerds mingling and worshipping the God of the chip, Mr. Kord himself. Christ, Dad, we even drink wine from a vineyard where the grapes are picked and pressed by machines that were programmed by a couple of Cybronics guys. The stuff tastes like Mister Clean, to tell you the truth."

I affixed a strip of tissue to my cheek, post-shaving style.

Sky smiled.

"Look, Sky, all I saw when you were there was some socializing and some discussion with Avery Kord on the monitor. About your various projects."

"The group consists of the top two hundredths of a percent in the company, I.Q.-wise," Sky said. "Our projects are the most important. Most of us head up programming teams and have other assignments as well; in my case, nobody on my team even knows about this project. I might ask them on occasion to come up with little bits of code, but I'm the one with the big picture. Because Avery Kord trusts me. And he trusts the other people I was meeting with in New York."

"Look, Sky, I met with Scarlett. She told me about this woman working opposite you. The one assigned to develop the subliminal suggestion program."

"I don't even know who she is. Planned anonymity. That's to insure that our work is based on research, on logic, rather than something we say to each other. It keeps the research pristine. It's a security precaution Avery takes."

"Well, her name's Kate."

His expression was blank.

"Katie Wilnot," I said. "From Orlando."

Sky's eyes lit up, as if I had just mentioned Mozart or Darwin or Van Gogh.

"Katie Wilnot's known as one of the best software architects in the world, Dad. They say she can remember sequences of hundreds of numbers more easily than most people can recall the words to The Star Spangled Banner. If what you say is true, I should be honored to be working opposite her."

I suddenly felt saltwater well up in my eyes as my throat got tense and the bowline knot in my stomach twisted and tightened.

"Scarlett was afraid of it all, Sky. So I went back to the church and I saw Katie there. Talking to Kord. I didn't hear all of it, but it sounded like Kord wants to test Katie's program with someone's life."

"What?"

"If I understood what I was hearing, he wanted to use the program to plant subliminal suggestions to a person to make that person go off and kill himself. As a test to see how convincing it can be, is what Kord said. Before using it on a terrorist like Saddam Hussein."

"Dad, this will sound weird, but we say crazy stuff like that all the time around here. It's only half-serious. It's exaggeration. Hyperbole. Makes the humdrum seem more exciting. But suicide isn't something any subliminal suggestion software could ever really make anybody commit. The survival instinct is far too strong, even in a depressed person. And knowing Avery, he was just trying to sound Katie out, maybe prompt her to think of a great test. When she does, he'll thank her and say he was kidding."

"Well, Katie's not going to be thinking of any test, Sky. She took pills. A lot of them. I don't know if it's because she was frightened and depressed or because she somehow got the program used on her. Maybe she decided to test it with her own life rather than sacrifice somebody else. She tried to do something with it at a seminar she taught out in California, to get people to change their opinions of Cybronics. But Kord said that's not enough of a test. Now she's in a coma. So to finish developing that program, Kord's going to need someone very familiar with it. Someone at her level."

My son turned as white as the monitor screen next to him and his lower lip twitched.

"You're not just talking, Dad. You're saying something."

"I'm certainly trying." I took his hand in mine and held it until some color returned to his cheeks.

"Dad, I'm happy. I finally found a niche I fit into. I love computers and programming and working crazy nighttime hours to meet deadlines and all the oddball people that populate this industry. One guy eats nothing but Ring Dings. With ketchup to make them a balanced diet. You're not allowed to smoke in the building, but there's a guy who's drilled a hole through his office wall; he sticks a cigarette holder through it and lights up outside his window. One woman never drinks a Coke without a Diet Coke to go with it. I could go on and on. What makes it all work is that they're all smart and they're all dedicated. And I even get a kick out of Avery and the famous megalomaniacal streak that the media is certain he has."

"He's frightening, Sky. Congress doesn't just keep investigating him for no reason. He abuses his power, his money. Crushes his competitors like aluminum cans. And there's that old story about his partner who was murdered. There's something odd, Sky. Anybody that power hungry—"

"He's just an overgrown spoiled kid, Dad. An ice-cream freak, for God's sake. And the stories about his past—they're too crazy to be true. He's always been great to me." Sky nodded, as if to convince himself. "Don't let old folk tales scare you."

"But you tried suicide once, Sky. We've been through so much. You're playing with fire here. I just don't want—"

"That all was a million light years ago. My perspective was off. I had a chemical imbalance or something. Like a disease I was cured of."

"So now I'm supposed to trust your resistance? Against a program designed precisely to pierce through a person's free will? When one person already seems to have given in?"

He looked at the floor.

"Avery would never be involved in what you're saying, Dad. And I would never, ever—" His denials had the ring of a person's I once met at the only AA meeting I ever attended.

"Look, I know you wouldn't do it voluntarily, consciously," I said. "But now with Katie unable to continue, he's going to want you to finish creating that subliminal suggestion software. You shouldn't do it, Sky. Stall. Delay. Do something to avoid it. And maybe you should just quit. There are still lots of high-tech companies you could work for, the remaining Dot Coms and what have you. Silicon Valley is full of them. Or Boston. You know a lot, Sky. Probably more than Avery Kord wants you to."

"Come on, Dad. Don't be Chicken Little. This isn't that old television show with Angela Lansbury."

"*Murder, She Wrote*," I said, smiling, remembering how I once got upset when Sky interrupted me during the denouement. He still knew just what to say to affect my mood.

Sky laughed and nodded, then spoke louder. "You've got to admit, Dad, a suggestion of suicide—fight it off or die—that would be the ultimate test of the program's ability to convince, wouldn't it? Man against machine. I kind of like the idea."

"I can't even think in those terms. It isn't funny. Your life's worth more than any test."

"Of course, Dad. I just meant it hypothetically." His voice got lower, cracked. "Look, Mom died trying to save me. I'd never let her down by making her death a waste." He kissed me on the unscratched cheek. "Why don't you get some sleep? I have to go to the office early tomorrow. Stop thinking morbid thoughts. And remember, people like to shoot arrows at the king."

I clasped my son's hands tightly.

"You think he was ever involved in really bad stuff like his partner's murder, Sky?"

"You mean that old rumorazzi nonsense about Justin Webb?" Sky frowned and shook his head. "Don't believe every piece of tabloid crap you read, Dad. Avery's the easiest scapegoat around. He was miles away when it happened."

"Maybe. But is it true he got agitated when he found out you were hacking around in an effort to prove that?"

"Scarlett again, Dad. You have what I call Scarlett Fever."

"Is it?" I pointed at the fading red gash on his temple. "Looks nasty."

He nodded. "It's not because I tried to find the killer. It's how. I was hacking. Avery doesn't want one of his key employees to do something dumb like getting caught breaking and entering into somebody else's database. That's what hacking really is. Or cracking. Bad for the corporate image."

"So is throwing a box of diskettes."

"An accident, Dad. He just meant to push them off a shelf."

"Maybe. But I thought you computer guys do that hacking and cracking stuff all the time."

"Not the top people, Dad. Too risky. According to Avery, anyway. And I have to agree, with the big Congressional investigation looming, it wouldn't be a good time to get caught breaking into somebody's database."

I took a deep breath. I hoped my genius son was right, but my comfort level was about as high as my ankles.

"Did you find anything?" I asked. "When you hacked?"

"Not really." He didn't hesitate, and his voice sounded more even. "I didn't get too far. All I got was a name. Henry Driver. The police could never pin it on him. I found some old records that identified him as someone they spoke to. But they never made his name public."

"Henry Driver?"

"A drifter or something."

I looked deeply into my son's eyes. They studied me the way Eliza's used to.

"I just want your promise, Sky. That you won't do anything stupid."

"You have it."

"Scout's honor?"

"I always thought that was silly, Dad. I never was a scout."

I remained silent, motionless. When Sky was a child, a minute or so of quiet stillness was all it took to get him to ease up and give in. Not so now.

He simply stood up and walked out of the room. Then I heard his bedroom door close and latch.

I wished I had a bottle of Dewar's, partly because I wanted to get smashed and partly to feel the emotional release of smashing it against a wall. Instead, I stared out the window at the large crescent that glowed white in the distance, a second moon in a sky that was black but starting to redden with the dawn. I wondered when the crescent would start tightening its grip like a claw around the weakened throat of my fragile existence. Or around my son's.

And I wondered just what I would do to stop it.

CHAPTER 18

"Welcome to the Cybronics campus," said the tour guide, standing in a disk-drive shaped doorway that led into Building Three, the third from the left in a horseshoe-shaped cluster of putty-colored buildings surrounding a sculpture garden. Having seen it all on 60 Minutes and in postcards, it seemed surreal when blown up to its actual dimensions. The tour guide was pony-tailed, mustached, puka-shelled, tie-dyed, bell-bottomed, looks that reminded me of David Crosby or Neil Young, I forget which. Except that he was cleaner than I imagined the rockers were, his skin sported a surfer's radiance, his features were sharp and symmetrical. Maybe a young Sonny Bono. His movements were a bit slow, his pronunciations deliberate, as if his voice had been fed through a synthesizer that transformed it into a southern drawl without the accent. Something about his expression seemed mechanical as well.

He handed me a white credit-card sized plastic card with Lightman, Clifford, and a series of numbers embossed across it.

"It's good only. For today," he said, his speech oddly broken. "You'll need it. To access. Certain areas. You can use it. At any Public Info. Terminal. You see." I glanced around and saw one a few feet away. It looked like an ATM.

"Great idea," I said, slipping the card into my shirt pocket.

"Of course," said the tour guide, smiling, straight pearly teeth reflecting a glimmer of the halogen glow from the ceiling. "You'll be with a group. Of four. Mr. Lightman. They're in. The waiting area. Please. Wait while I get them. And we'll all. Get going."

I looked around as he walked over to a glassed-in room. The plant was huge, and much of it was a wide open central space. Workers in white astronaut-style suits moved slowly about in several rooms that had walls of glass like the waiting room. Offices full of glowing computer monitors lined the perimeter.

"Dust," the tour guide said, suddenly behind me. I jumped.

"Sorry," he continued. "The suits and. The glass. Protect against dust. A hair, a little bit. Of. Skin. A drop. Of mucus. Anything as small as a. Micron. Can ruin. A perfectly good piece. Of software. Or hardware. Even a great one. Like. Me."

"You mean you're—" two of the guests blurted out simultaneously.

"A computer?" the tour guide asked. "A robot? If not here, where? If not now. When?"

"You're amazing!" one of the women said. She wore a crimson sweatshirt with a big "H" on the front and looked a bit beyond college age; maybe a grad student.

"If Manhattan were. A micron," the tour guide continued, seeming unfazed, "it would fit. On the head. Of a pin. We also have. Air filters. That can nail germs. That small." He smiled and the woman nodded back.

Our little group followed the tour guide past some workrooms, his arms and knees noticeably stiffer than ours as he shuffled along. We watched employees manipulate tiny items with robotized hands and fingers, which they controlled with computer mice and remote controls while staring at a magnifying monitor.

"The assembly area," the guide said. "These technicians are. The assembly line. Workers of today. As unskilled. As it gets. In this. Industry."

"How much do they make?" a man in a blue business suit with white sneakers asked.

"Fifty dollars," the guide said. "An hour."

"That's not too unskilled," the graduate student said.

"You should apply," said the guide. "We often need. More help. As we expand."

"I always see Cybronics on t.v., in the magazines," the other woman said in a shy mousy voice. "But I'm not sure exactly what this company is."

"At Cybronics, we make life worth living," droned the tour guide.

"Well, what does that mean, in terms of products?" asked the businessman in sneakers. "For instance, with IBM, we think of hardware. Intel makes chips. Microsoft makes operating systems and software. Just what does Cybronics specialize in?"

"The cutting. Edge," said the guide. "Improving upon. What's already out there. Hardware. Software. Chips. Browsers. The shell—that's the interface. Whatever it takes. To bring. A particular. Concept to life."

The other guests looked as puzzled as I felt.

The tour guide elaborated.

"We don't just start. With the idea. That we'll make hardware. Or software. Or microprocessors," he said. "That's how other. Manufacturers. Operate. At Cybronics, we think. Of a concept. Then we do whatever. It takes. To bring it. Into existence. In the cheapest. Most efficient. Most reliable manner. Isn't that right, Avery?"

"It is," chuckled the adolescent voice of Avery Kord. I didn't see him, or any speakers or cameras, either. His voice continued.

"I've been listening, and please allow me to answer you. We conceptualize first, then create. Think of people as cavemen who are tired of eating raw flesh. We dream of cooked meat. Then we invent fire and the barbecue and the utensils to go with it. But if someone's already carved out that specialty, we consider ways to make it hotter or safer or easier to use. Some of our main areas include arts and entertainment, consumer electronics, databases, education, networks, news—not to mention professional software of all kinds, the net, television, travel. We're up there in all areas."

"But where are you yourself, Mr. Kord?" the grad student asked. "I mean physically, right now."

"I'm all around you," came the disembodied reply. "You're in my little playground, where I see all and hear all. But now I need to run to a meeting. So keep paying close attention to my electronic friend. Nice meeting you all!"

My brow furrowed as I looked at the tour guide. The Sonny Bono look-a-like shrugged and stared blankly. Just past him, I noticed a Public Info terminal. I scrambled up to it and inserted my card.

An ATM-like display quickly lit up and words appeared in white on blue:

How may I help you, Mr. Lightman? Touch one bar, please:
1. Provide more information about Cybronics.
2. Provide more information about Cybronics personnel.
3. Explain how a particular item works.
4. Location of the nearest convenience stop.

I touched bar number 2, and a new menu appeared:

1. How many employees does Cybronics have?
2. How diverse are we?
3. How educated is our work force?
4. What are our names?
5. How to apply for a position.

Not seeing anything specific about Kord, I pushed a fire-red icon labeled Exit. The screen went blank.

"I'm sure you'd. All like. Some lunch," the tour guide said as I rejoined the group.

"Actually, I'd like to visit my son," I said. "Schuyler Lightman."

The tour guide seemed to think for a moment, then said, "He's in. Special R&D. Up on Six."

I turned to walk to the elevators, but the guide quickly grabbed my arm with a vise-like grip.

"You can't go. Unescorted. But he has. Something planned. For you. After lunch." My arm was red when he let it go.

I don't remember either the food or the conversation, but both reminded me of cardboard. The mechanized Sonny Bono, of course, didn't eat. He was lucky.

After lunch, a rest stop and a few more glass-walled rooms, he left me in the custody of a lab-coated guard built like a bouncer. We walked into the elevator and turned toward the door. The guard pressed Six and stared straight ahead. We got out and walked past a row of offices lined with computer terminals. Then past a man who was gesturing in front of a full-length mirror and a wall of monitors, most of which were tracking the other guests on my tour and the downstairs surroundings. The man wore a white suit that stuck to his skin like scuba gear, with wires coming out of electrodes that were affixed to it at numerous places—the wrists, upper arms, shoulders, thighs, calves; similar, smaller wires were attached to large vinyl gloves on his hands and boots on his feet. The wires all led into a bank of computers attached to controls he was also working, along with several joysticks and buttons. A camera also seemed to be focused on his face; his expressions were duplicated in real time on a small monitor screen—on an animated version of the tour guide's face. The man spoke into a microphone headset, and when I heard his familiar nasal voice and the odd. Way. He. Broke up. His sentences, it left me with no doubt that his bodily and facial movements and speech were being replicated by the tour guide downstairs. Sonny Bono wasn't a walking, talking, independently thinking robot at all, but a remote-controlled mannequin, a life-size marionette with a wired-up puppeteer.

The guard dropped me off at the Holography Laboratory. We didn't speak a word to one another in the two long minutes we were together. He pushed a green button outside the door and it slid open. I walked in and the door slid closed behind me.

The Holography Lab looked like many of the glassed-in rooms I had seen downstairs, full of monitors and terminals, but it also had some antique furnishings and a beautiful old Persian rug in its center.

"Pretty cool, huh, Dad?" Schuyler said, getting up from behind a terminal.

"The rug?"

"No. The company tour."

"It is, Sky. Especially when Avery Kord just drops in unexpectedly. By voice, I mean."

"He does that to employees, too. You never know when or where he'll turn up. Voice, or image, or in the flesh. But you get used to it."

"Sounds like Big Brother."

"It's okay, Dad. Trust me. Avery's great."

Especially when he's listening, I thought, but I kept my mouth shut and smiled instead.

"You like the tour guide, Dad?"

"He didn't eat much in the cafeteria."

Sky laughed. "I designed some of his circuits. Someday he'll be a fully automated computer, but for now we just have fun faking it. I've worn the control suit myself."

"Just like the man behind the curtain in The Wizard of Oz."

He walked back over to the terminal and sat on a stool in front of it. He banged out keystrokes faster than Elton John playing Pinball Wizard on the electric piano. Then he stood up again and walked over next to me on the rug.

"You came all the way out to Portland to celebrate Mom.ava, Dad."

"Right."

"So I thought Mom should be part of the celebration. Like I told you, the Mom.ava program's like a website. I can access it and bring her here."

Sky took my hand and led me off the rug, to a corner near the sliding door. He dimmed the lights slightly and took a remote control off of a rack on the wall. He hit a button and the rug rolled up, seemingly by itself, to reveal that it had been covering a small metal pod. An identical pod descended from the ceiling until it hung like a lighting fixture directly above its twin.

Sky pressed another button on the remote and a swirling kaleidoscope of laser lights shot from the top pod to the bottom one.

"What's the password, Dad?"

"The password?"

"To the Mom.ava program. The auditory receptors are waiting. I've got her programmed to respond only to your voice."

Newly metamorphosed butterflies flitted around in my stomach and goosebumps rose up on my skin.

"Shutterbug," I thought I said, but obviously in too mild a voice.

"What, Dad?"

"Shutterbug!" I repeated, louder, my emotions reliving what they had felt that night when I pulled out the diamond ring in the Mexican restaurant and asked Eliza to marry me.

She had hesitated back then, and I glared at her wide-eyed.

"What're you staring at?" she had said then, with a sly smile, before breaking into laughter because she knew what the answer would be.

"What're you staring at?" the hologram said now, and it was Eliza, life-size, three-dimensional, in the same old white cardigan and jeans she wore back then. And the ever-present pearls. She started laughing.

"Both of you, what? Do I look fat or something?"

I looked at Sky. He smiled back.

"How you feeling, Mom?" he asked the 3-D image of his mother, his tone as matter-of-fact as if she were merely getting over a cold.

"I feel pretty well, Sky," she replied, nodding. "Now are we here to celebrate, or what?"

"You got it, Mom." Schuyler walked over to a faded old globe and flipped open the top half. Out of the southern hemisphere came a bottle of wine, a can of Coke, three glasses and a corkscrew.

"Cliff, you do the honors," Eliza said. "Watching you open a bottle of wine will remind me of NYU."

I complied and poured three glasses. Sky winked as I bypassed the wine to fill his glass with Coke. I handed it to him, picked up my own glass and left Eliza's on the floor. The image of a glass identical to ours appeared in her hand, half-full, as if she had just taken it from me.

"To us," I said, and raised my glass.

"All of us," said Sky, raising his.

"The Lightmans," said Eliza. She polished off her wine before mine reached my lips.

"Nice bouquet," she said.

"You never drank that quickly, Lize," I said. "We didn't even clink."

"You're right," she said. "I guess I was excited." After a short pause, the image of her glass refilled halfway.

"One more toast," said Sky. "Of course, Mom, we can't really clink with you."

"To Avery Kord, who made this all possible," Eliza said. I wondered if she meant it or had said it because she thought Kord might be eavesdropping.

Sky reached over to clink with me. I didn't budge. Sky must have slipped, and he knocked over the third glass I had poured. The glass toppled and the wine splashed out over the black pod.

"Shit!" Eliza said, loudly, an electronic fizz in her voice, and suddenly her image looked charred before it began to smoke and then black out.

"Shit is right!" Sky said, his voice trembling as he fumbled with the remote control before hitting a few buttons. "I just shorted out the hologram projector!"

"How big a problem is it, Sky?"

"They'll fix it. It'll take a day or two. But now I'll have to explain it. Mom.ava's my own program. Not approved by Cybronics. You're not supposed to run unapproved software in the building."

"So you'll have to tell Avery Kord?"

He stared at the floor. "There are sensors in various strategic places to detect problems. So they'll know something happened up here. But Avery's pretty forgiving, Dad."

"What about Mom.ava?"

"I hope she's okay. But we didn't exit properly. We'll just have to try to boot her up somewhere else and keep our fingers crossed. In the meantime, I'd better make sure I didn't royally fuck the place up."

"Be careful, Sky," I said. He nodded and waved as the door slid open and another stonefaced guard appeared to escort me back to the elevator.

CHAPTER 19

I had just gotten settled in Sky's apartment when he called to tell me he'd be home in the middle of the night, if at all. He had to run more tests to be certain the accident in the Holography Lab didn't release any potential bugs into Cybronics' central computer systems. He told me to make myself comfortable, so I tried.

I sat at his desk and was about to log on to his home computer when I noticed part of a little rose design on a sheet of paper sticking out from under the keyboard. I pulled it out and unfolded it. It was Scarlett Exner's personal stationery, and on it she had written an undated note in a rounded, childlike script:

Dear Sky,
I know you prefer e-mail, but I didn't want to give you the option of just hitting "delete." It takes more effort to crumple a piece of paper and toss it into the garbage.
Words cannot express the love I will always feel for you, despite what has come between us. I place no blame on either of us. People sometimes grow apart.
Please believe me when I tell you I want to help you. I am in an awkward position—you know what I mean—but it also enables me to know a few things. And I beg you to be careful. You're fooling around with dynamite. One day some scientists scratch out a set of equations on a blackboard, the next day there's a mushroom cloud. Theory is nice, but how it's applied is really all that matters. And human motives are not always obvious, even to a genius like you. Perhaps especially to one.
I hope I'm making sense. This is all way over my head (despite Yale!). Just remember that no matter what happens, you can always trust and

count on me.
  Love sincerely,
  S.E.

I refolded the note and placed it back under the keyboard. It didn't seem to refer to anything Scarlett hadn't shared with me. But that suggested to me that her professed discomfort was sincere. Although I hoped her perception was inaccurate, I strongly doubted it.

I wiped some sweat off my hands and switched on Sky's home computer. I was still light years from being computer-proficient, and it took me hours to boot up Eliza and say "Shutterbug." I was surprised that she remembered our last experience. She seemed no worse for wear.

"That was a close one, Cliff," she said. "Kids shouldn't fool around with lasers. I'm happy enough in two dimensions."

"But it sure was fun in 3-D while it lasted, Lize."

"There's always virtual reality, Cliff. For a hot time, call me up on it. You'll need a full-body sensation suit and one of those VR headsets. And a condom. I wouldn't want you to get electrocuted."

"You putting me on?"

She smiled and laughed. I'd always thought of computers as cold pieces of equipment. Perhaps I had been wrong.

"You haven't talked to him yet, Cliff. Have you?"

"A little bit. He insists everything's okay. I was planning to have another heart-to-heart tonight, Lize, but because of the accident—"

"They're keeping him late?"

I nodded.

"Listen, Cliff. After the spill, the program I'm in—it didn't shut off. I was still alive, in a sense. Conscious. And I snuck into the system at Cybronics."

"The word is 'sneaked,' Lize. Or more accurately, trespassed. You broke and entered."

"And who's going to put me in jail?"

"You have a point, Lize. But how can you be conscious once you've—once Mom.ava, I mean—has been turned off?"

"Well, I wasn't turned off properly. And somehow—I don't know, Sky and you, your input, I mean, you somehow recreated my consciousness. My feelings. Sky input all that old film, all the photographs, the video, you guys put in all that personality stuff, so somehow I have vivid memories—"

"I can't pretend to understand how."

"Does it matter?"

I shook my head from side to side and smiled. It didn't. "So, what did you find?"

"I got into some of Avery Kord's computer files. I didn't have time to read them or decipher them. They're encrypted. In some kind of code I can't figure out. I'll need to search for the decoding program. But I made copies of a handful that seemed relevant."

"You have a camera?"

"I have whatever equipment I need to capture bits of info, Cliff. You can visualize it as a camera. That's how I think about it. A Canon EOS-1N. So, truth be told, I can scan electronic files pretty quickly and photograph the interesting ones. I clone them, actually, and keep the clone. The originals stay in their files."

"How could you tell which ones seemed relevant?"

"Well, that was a tough decision, Cliff, and I'm not sure I'm right. I scanned them very quickly. But the file names weren't in code, and"—she had an odd smirk on her face—"I had a pretty good guess which ones to copy."

"Which?"

"The ones labeled 'Lightman.'"

CHAPTER 20

The aroma of roasted coffee awakened me from a deep sleep. It was rich, earthy, reminded me of mornings in the sunroom peering into Eliza's nightgown as she bent to pour it. Something I never tired of.

It was made automatically, I realized, kind of a coffee alarm clock Sky must have set for me. But it was already noon. I poured a cup and downed it, black, in two gulps. Then I poured another.

I called Sky's office to find out what his plans were for the day. A polite computer-driven female voice informed me that the number I had reached was out of service or had been temporarily disconnected. I tried again to be sure. Same message.

I downed my second cup, turned the machine off, tossed on some clothes and headed quickly out on the road for Cybronics. My foot felt like a lead weight on the gas pedal as I shot down street after street of well-tended houses and manicured lawns. I didn't know what I'd do if I hit a red light. Or maybe I went through a few, to tell you the truth, and almost clipped a tourist trolley car to boot.

Once I reached the Cybronics campus, it took an argument and proof in the form of the previous day's Public Info terminal card to get past the guard at the parking lot gate. I was no longer an invited guest. I almost got lost in a maze of hedges and modern sculptures—mostly big red metal structures that looked like giant rabbits from the left or giant wolves from the right—but I made my way over to Building Three and double-checked the number before walking in. I was told to wait at reception.

The puka-shelled bell-bottomed tour guide came up and greeted me.

"I'm here to see my son," I said.

"Just what is your name, sir," the guide asked in a smooth baritone, "and what is your son's?"

"Look, whoever controls this tour guide today," I shouted into the air, "up on the sixth floor, why not scan your computers? I was here yesterday. And I'd like to talk to you in the flesh."

A pause as the machine's eyes moved upward, leftward. The man upstairs was making the machine look like it was thinking. "The relevant data has been deleted, sir," it finally said.

I grabbed the machine's lapels and pulled it toward me. My knuckles pressed against its chest. It felt colder than it looked, rubbery but lined underneath with tendony wire cables. It raised its hands between my arms, then pushed down and out with each, breaking my grip. Assumed a stance I recalled from Sky's futile childhood attempts to earn a green belt.

"I do not advise you to try that again, sir," the tour guide announced in a calm tone. "Now, what is your name, and what is your son's?"

The skin of my face was on fire, my eyes searing as they narrowed. I had trouble comprehending what was going on.

Two large security guards walked toward me from opposite ends of the glassed-in reception area, metal badges reflecting glints of light. Beyond the glass, I saw three people who appeared to be waiting for a tour like the one I had taken. One shot me a sneer, obviously intended to convey that it was my fault for delaying their day's agenda. I was plainly an unexpected disturbance.

"My name's Lightman," my voice said, seeming to have done so on its own and without the cooperation of my tight scratchy throat. "Cliff Lightman," it continued. "I need to see my son, Schuyler. I was here yesterday." My hand reached into my shirt pocket, pulled out the Public Info terminal card and handed it to one of the guards.

"Minute." He walked over to a nearby Public Info terminal. I followed and watched as he inserted my card. The display read EXPIRED. Then he removed my card and inserted another. The familiar screen menu appeared. He punched up WHAT ARE OUR NAMES? and an employee list appeared. The guard scrolled down to the L's: Licht, Lichtenstein, Lido, Liddy, Lifschutz, Liggett, Ligurian.

"No Lightman," the guard finally said. "I assume you spell it like light bulb, speed of light, that sort of thing."

"This is impossible."

"You saw it yourself. Sure he hasn't changed it?"

My head felt ready to explode. I still had a red gash on my cheek and figured I looked tough. I wanted to fight one of these guys, draw blood. But I figured they probably didn't have any.

"I need to see Avery Kord," I said. "Immediately. It's important business."

"Fraid that's impossible, sir." Puka shells moved up and down in unison with the tour guide's latex Adam's apple.

"You don't understand. Something's terribly wrong."

"We do understand, sir. But Mister Kord never has unscheduled visitors."

"Specially when he's out of town," one of the guards grunted. They all chuckled and repeated his punch line as if doing so made it funnier.

"When's he coming back?" I asked.

"That won't change the net result," the tour guide replied. "But if you're interested, I think he's scheduled to return a week from Friday."

"I need to leave a message with his secretary."

"You just did, sir," a shrewish Lily Tomlinesque "one ringy dingy" voice assured me from an unplaceable direction. "It's Clifford Lightman, New York, New York. We've got your number, sir. I'll have Mr. Kord call at his earliest convenience. He's away working on a special short term project, but he checks in."

"But I'm not going to be in New York. I'm staying at my son's place in Portland."

"Your son? What is his name, sir?"

"Come on, lady. He works here! In special R&D up on six!"

"I'm very sorry, Mister Lightman, but we have no one on file here with your last name. Are you sure it isn't Leighton?"

"I'm going to call the police," I said.

"If it makes you feel better, sir, you can do so from reception. Charles, why don't you hand Mister Leighton—Mister Lightman—a cellular?"

One of the guards unclipped a cell phone from his belt, handed it to me. I started to dial, thought about it, handed it back.

"I'm leaving," I announced.

"Have a nice day," the tour guide called after me.

I started up the rented Taurus but I didn't know where to head. Downtown? I had a tourist map of Portland with a number and address for a police station. Q-14, the lower right quadrant. Southeast. I started driving, looked for a pay phone. Then thought I'd try Sky's apartment again. It was on the way. This had to be some kind of mistake.

Or a joke. Sky wasn't beyond a sophomoric prank or two, I tried to reassure myself. Nerdy geniuses love that kind of stuff. I couldn't remember him playing any gags on me, but I was his father so how could I expect otherwise? Perhaps this was an attempt to make light of our late night/early morning discussion, make me realize how silly I was to worry about him. Or how wrong to spy. I just wanted to hug him and apologize and promise to stay out of matters above my head. What did I know about web servers and programming language and Congressional antitrust hearings? I should stick to my customer complaints and polite response letters and reviews of outside law firm bills.

I zipped along Route 26 and across a bridge. Sky lived near an historical old pedestrian magnet called the Pittock Mansion, which took an eternity to drive by, even though it was high up on a hill. A light rain was falling and I felt damp and uncomfortable against the leatherette seats.

When I finally reached the apartment building, I skipped the elevator, raced up five flights, quickly opened the door with Schuyler's keypad code. The butterfly chairs and gray Formica table my son thought of as antiques were in their familiar places, and even the faint fresh-roasted java scent lingered in the air. Mount Hood still sat in the snow-capped postcard view out the living room window. I wasn't losing my mind. But there were several cameras and film canisters and various sizes of lenses on the table and a camera bag on the floor, none of which had been there earlier. It was all high-end equipment, Canon and Nikon components I might have mistaken for Eliza's at first glance, but it all had a rubbed out, almost second-hand quality. Eliza took better care of her stuff.

I heard voices from the bedroom. Male and female. Lighthearted banter, gibberish I couldn't quite make out. A giggle. I removed my shoes and tiptoed on the carpet toward the door. No keyhole, not enough space under the door to see anything. Wrong angle, anyway. Couldn't tell if it was Sky.

A cellular phone sat on the table. I picked it up, turned it on, dialed Sky's apartment, the same number I had called at least once a week for two years.

I stared at the wallphone, expected it to ring. It didn't. The cell phone indicated the line was ringing, but the apartment phones were silent.

Another kind woman computer voice. Another message that another phone was out of service or had been temporarily disconnected.

I turned off the cellphone, replaced it on the table and began knocking on the bedroom door.

The voices inside went silent, then started up again in a faint whisper. I knocked again.

"Yeah. Who is it?" Male. Deep.

"Cliff Lightman," I said. "Is Sky in there?"

"Who?"

"Sky. Schuyler Lightman."

The door opened. The voice's owner stood in the doorway, shirt off, chest matted with graying hair covering big square pects. Pajama bottoms inside out. Huge biceps I didn't want to offend, the left one tattooed with a skull and crossbones in a burning fire. In the background, on the bed, large bobbing breasts were being quickly covered by a geometric Mondrian quilt. Definitely human, flesh, not latex or even silicone. The saline smell of sweat overcame the remaining odor of the morning's coffee.

"He's my son and this is his apartment," I said.

"You're fucking crazy," the man said. "We been living here three years come Friday."

"That's impossible."

"Don't you fucking tell me what's possible in my own fucking house," the man said.

"Take it easy, Hank," the woman said, voice trembling. I wondered if she was afraid of me or afraid of what her tattooed companion's biceps might do to me.

"Shut up, Tammy," Hank said without turning, still staring at me. "So how'd you get in here?"

"With the code. I told you—"

"How'd you know my fucking door code, anyway? You a devil worshipper or something?"

"He must've read *The Exorcist* too, Hank," Tammy called out from the bed.

"Look, Mister, let's just call a truce and you leave peaceful-like. I got a .45 Magnum and practice usin' it."

"Only thing he can shoot straight is his wad," Tammy shouted, and I began to wonder whether she had a death wish.

"I said shut the fuck up," Hank screamed, glancing at Tammy, opening and closing his fists as if to get them ready. "I can aim straight enough to blow you another orifice where your brain used to be."

"Look, maybe this was a mistake," I said. Guns always made me shiver. "But the code was also my son's."

"3845 Lovejoy Street, apartment 3-A?" he asked.

"Yup. You have a computer, Hank?"

"A Magnum ain't exactly a computer, Mister."

"I know that, Hank. I just want to know if you have one."

"You came here to steal it?"

"No. But if you have one, maybe I can show you—"

"You playin' fuckin' games with me?" The cords in his neck tightened, knotted.

"Hank—" Tammy pleaded, sitting up, less self-conscious, nightgown still balled up on the floor two feet from the bed, blanket twisted so there wasn't enough surface area to cover all her parts, trying to decide which to hide. For the first time I noticed a video camera on a folded tripod leaning against a corner on the far side of the bed. It was plainly off, though it seemed obvious what they must have been filming before I arrived.

"It's okay, Babe. This guy's outta here."

"Why do you think I'm playing games, Hank?" I asked.

"Cause I had a razzle-dazzle state-of-the-art machine in here this morning," he said, "and the fucker somehow got stolen sometime between then and half an hour ago. Worth twenty grand if it was worth a nickel. Not to mention the stuff I had stored in the memory."

"You looked for it half an hour ago?"

"Had to, Mister," Tammy said from the bed, her upper lip twitching. "We look at kids on the Internet to get us started."

"I said shut the fuck up!" Hank, purple-faced, with a predatory expression, turned and ran to her, yanked the blanket off and twisted it around her neck, pulled it tight. She made a gurgling noise as she tugged at it, knuckles white, eyes in a wide scare. He must have let up his grip because she went flying backward over the bed, feet over her head, a thud made by her naked legs and bruised black-and-blue buttocks as they hit the floor. She must have grazed the legs of the tripod because it tipped over, the video camera's fall to the floor broken by her upper back.

"Get out, Mister," Hank yelled, and I could see rage in his eyes as his biceps and his crotch both swelled for use in some fashion on this woman. I was afraid he might kill her and I wanted to stop him or call the police immediately; but, as I often explained to subway panhandlers on my lousier days, I had my own problems. I had walked into this movie in the middle and had no idea what had come before. Besides, I figured, when I went to the police about Sky and retraced my steps, they'd find these creeps on their own.

"Don't worry, Mister," the woman called out, shaking it all off, reading my mind as I started to leave. "That little spat turned Hank on, just as good as a nine-year-old spreading it out all over the screen." Then, obviously to Hank: "Ain't that right, Babe? You ready now?"

Some people forgive way too easily.

I headed for the police station.

CHAPTER 21

"Isn't a missing person until he's missing," the sergeant said, politely, removing his thumbs from behind his red suspenders. His office stank of stale Marlboros despite the Thank You for Not Smoking plaque planted on the front of his desk near his computer monitor. "Out here, that means 48 hours, Mister, Sir. Minimum." He used one forefinger the size of a cigar to tap a few keys on his keyboard terminal.

"But he's not just missing," I said, trying to reason. "He's been abducted. Erased."

"Imaginative." He nodded, scratched an oversized Jay Leno chin that somehow made him seem nicer than he probably was. "But what do I have to go on, Ay?"

"Everything I just explained to you. Cybronics. The address."

"Now, now, Mister, Sir. Any problem ever occurs out here, first thing everybody says is Cybronics. Car accident? The computer chip that runs the vehicle was defective, let's blame Cybronics. Plane late? Cybronics software runs air traffic control. Bad weather? Cybronics programs not only should have predicted it down at the meteorological station, they should have changed it. Christ, when a kid died last year from eating a bad hamburger from that—you know, the e. colon stuff, the bacteria—do they picket the fast food joint that undercooks the darned patty? Heck, no! They picket Cybronics for not programming the oven to override the mistakes made by the pimply high school kids behind the counter. Somebody in this town cuts the cheese, it's gotta be Cybronics' fault. Well, lemme tell ya something, Ay? I got four kids grew up in this town, and two of 'em work out there at the Big C. They make pretty good money, and Mister Avery Kord himself sends me—not just my offspring, mind you, he sends me—a Christmas card. One of em's a little slow, too, if ya catch my driftwood, Mister, Sir. Finishes at the end a the race. Don't ya think Mister Avery Kord located a Portland boy a job out there at the C plant, whether the kid's a tortoise or a hare? Don't ya think them executives got cars need to be washed, just like yours and mine, Ay? And not mind it at all that they can park and go to work and when they come out to go home they got shiny polished fenders waiting for 'em, Ay, Mister, Sir?"

"But that's got nothing to do—"

"Look, my friend. I'm not tellin' ya I got any conflict a interest, Ay? Ya gotta trust me. We got search helicopters just like in the east. Somethin's wrong out there, I'll be first into the Big C with my gun blazing. Done it one time with one a them hermits, I did, ya know, can ya 'magine me aimin' right for the spot where a normal person's heart would be, but figurin' all along he probably ain't got one, ya know? Didn't matter after I pulled the trigger, it was gonna be me or him, and I sure wasn't gonna let it be me, no sir, Mister! But lemme tall ya, if I might share a personal anecdotal story, lemme be frank with ya. Even my own kid's been missing in life a day or two a time, yet he always shows up. Always shows up. Gets hungry eventually, ya know? Ain't never been kidnapped by Cybronics, Mister, Sir, even if sometimes he don't get the shine quite right or he puts a scratch on one a Mister Avery Kord's new Silver Clouds. Did it once, I swear. So trust me. That Skylight a yours—"

"Schuyler."

"That Schuyler, right, sorry, Ay? He's still gone day after tomorrow, we'll have us a missing person and a real case to pursue. A case, with a capital C, if ya follow. The kind where we haul out the searchlights and the infrareds and the bloodhounds. But he's not five or six, Mister Lightman, Sir. He's able-bodied, over twenty. Could have eloped, moved to Europe, joined a circus."

"Not Schuyler."

"But you catch my meaning."

I wasn't sure I did. I nodded anyway. "What about his apartment? Hank and Tammy being there and Sky being gone?"

"While we were sittin' here, Mister, Sir, I did a search, Mister Lightman. A real sophisticated database search, too. The latest state-of-the-art program. You saw me typing? Trust me, the famous blue N.Y.P.D. don't have such advanced equipment, Ay? It was a charitable gift to the Portland Police."

He knew what I was thinking and gave me an exaggerated wink. Then he motioned with his hand for me to come behind his desk, and I obliged. I looked at the screen and he pointed out some lines on his monitor.

"Ya see, Mister, Sir? Henry Driver and Tammy Wood have been living at that address ya gave me about three years. Ya see their descriptions, their socials, Ay? Driver's got a child porn arrest, but no conviction. Was a suspect in an old felony murder, too, but we couldn't pin it on him."

"Avery Kord's partner." It had taken me a few seconds, but I recalled the name of the suspect Schuyler said he'd found. Henry Driver.

"I can't confirm that one way or t'other," the Sergeant said. "Policy. You can't confirm or deny where a case can't be proven, Mister L. And I ain't even gonna ask you how you might've come to know that little fact that I can't confirm, you follow?"

I nodded and quickly decided not to volunteer anymore, certainly not to mention Sky's efforts in the area of computer hacking, but my pulse was pounding from the burden of my worst fears.

"Anyway," the Sergeant continued, "they sell smut over the Net, these two. Pictures a kids and stuff. These days a camera can be a dangerous weapon, Mister Lightman, Sir. But we'll catch their hairy butts one a these days, we will. We been after 'em. So I believe you were there, all right, at the apartment. You're credible on that score. And I'll send somebody over there to ask about your kid, but you can be sure Driver ain't about to let on if he knows something. And there's no record your son was ever there, or anywhere in Oregon for that matter."

"You have national records?"

"Most states don't keep up to date as well as we do, ya know. Our data is updated just about continuously. Fed in from the clerks' offices, the sheriff's, motor vehicles, all the right places." I sat back in my seat as he slowly typed in a few codes. "I do have something on your son."

"What?"

"Seems congratulations might be in order, Mister, Sir," he said, nodding. "He obviously got admitted into Yale—otherwise why would he be listed on College Street in New Haven, Connecticut?"

"He hasn't lived there since he graduated. Almost two years ago."

He held his hands out, palms up, and shrugged his shoulders. "Like I said, most states aren't as diligent as Oregon about updating their records," he said. "Now you take it easy, and if I see ya in 48 hours we'll have us a drink together for good luck and we'll open a file, Ay? Until then, try to relax."

"Easy for you to say."

"Hey, Mister, Sir, any kid's smart enough for Yale isn't gonna just let himself up and disappear. Especially not from beautiful Portland, Oregon. Once ya live in the City of Roses, Mister, Sir, ya want to stay here 'til ya die. Me, Sir, I came here thirty years ago, and where am I today? A rose by any other name, ya know? Says so on one a those concrete sidewalks outside, I'll betcha. Or something just the equivalent, from Shakespeare or somebody who wrote Shakespeare. You can trust me on that score."

CHAPTER 22

I left the police station and loosened my collar. I walked over to the public library I had noticed when I parked the car. A helpful old librarian who reminded me of Sky's third-grade teacher—or was it fourth?—smiled warmly as she fixed me up with a microfiche machine and miniaturized copies of the *Oregonian*. She was pretty certain the murder occurred in '82 or '83, because back then she lived up near a park in the northwest part of town, where she thought it occurred. I saw no reason to argue, so I started with those years. I scanned only the front pages, figuring it would have been headline news.

It occurred on April 14, 1982, and was deemed important enough by the editors to appear above smaller captions about last-minute tax filers and Frank Sinatra selling out the Center for Performing Arts:

LOCAL BUSINESSMAN SHOT TO DEATH

I leaned on my hand and could feel my pulse pounding through my carotid artery as I read the article on the screen. There was no by-line. At approximately 12:40 on a Wednesday afternoon, a man killed Justin Webb as he rode his 10-speed Peugeot racing bike along a quiet dirt path in Forest Park. According to the police, the assailant shot him twice: once while he was on the bike, knocking him off it; and a second time after he was down, at point blank range. Then the killer fled on the bike, which was found chained to a bike rack in a parking lot four miles from the scene. There was only one witness, a man who called 911 anonymously. He claimed he was sitting on a park bench about a hundred yards away. He described what happened and said he could see enough of the killer to identify him as Caucasian, but that was it.

By coincidence, only a few hours after Webb was shot, Avery Kord was being interviewed on a local business radio show. He received the news about his business partner while he was in the KNPB 1410 studio and abruptly ended the interview, but not before crying out, "Oh My God!" Those words, Kord's last in the studio, were loud enough to be picked up on the show even though the microphones had been turned off by then.

What struck me as odd was that Webb was killed at all. His wallet was left in his pocket. The assailant took the bike, but he could have taken it without shooting Webb a second time once he was down. Police speculated that Webb might have had some way of identifying his attacker. The bullet that sprayed his cerebrum over three wild rose bushes eliminated that possibility.

I read a few follow-up articles. They added some details about Webb's life: he was a workaholic who loved biking, chocolate and the computer company he founded with Avery Kord, Cybronics Partners, which went on, not long after his murder, to obtain its first major contract to supply IBM with a key component of the visual interface for its PC's. But if Avery Kord was suspected of somehow arranging the killing or worse, the police and the newspapers did quite a job of pretending otherwise. Rather, he was portrayed as heartbroken, grief-stricken, suicidal, worried about how he could carry on without his childhood friend. He was a pallbearer. A close-up picture of him holding up a corner of Webb's pine coffin, tears streaming down his cheeks, removed all doubt. He looked innocent. For a few months following the murder, he hired bodyguards to watch himself and his father and other members of his family.

A handful of suspects were questioned over the next year or two, but the police never released their names and there was too little evidence to charge anyone with the murder. I figured one of them was Henry Driver, whose name my son had discovered while hacking, but none of the articles even hinted at Driver's identity. The anonymous 911 call was traced to a pay phone in the center of the city; it had been wiped clean of prints.

The library got stuffy fast, so I thanked the librarian and strolled outside.

I sat down on a bench in a nearby pocket park and stared at the pigeons. I wondered whether they were cleaner than the ones in New York or if it was just my imagination. I needed the fresh air and some time to think. The light rain no longer bothered me, but felt cleansing as I meditated into the crystal clear water of a bubbling fountain.

Since the accident I had learned not to expect life to be fair. But in the three years that passed I had just managed to regain a semblance of normalcy, a veneer of a routine that enabled me to cling to a windowsill on the side of the vacant old building that had become my existence. Now I felt as if someone was stomping on my straining fingertips with army boots.

To leave Portland with Schuyler missing would be one of the most difficult decisions I ever made, but I wasn't sure he was there anyway, and I had to take steps to save him—steps I thought I could take better elsewhere. I hoped I wasn't already too late.

CHAPTER 23

During the flight home, I rested my head on one of the undersized airplane pillows and pulled a warm woolen blanket over my eyes, but I couldn't sleep and my heart wouldn't stop palpitating. It didn't help when I accepted the stewardess's offer of a free headset, only to discover Avery Kord and his computeristic vision of the future on one of the channels. I clutched my barf bag but felt compelled to listen to his scratchy voice crackle on about the dawning of a new age in which man and machine would merge into a fresh new ultra-productive super-easy existence.

According to Kord, your entire office—your entire life, actually—would fit into a little notebook. Whole novels, if not libraries, would be stored on wafer-thin disks you insert into a flexible 8" x 10" minicomputer with a white paper screen that would look and feel like a paperback, yet be sand and water-resistant enough to allow you to bring all your junky reads to the beach and your Encyclopedia Britannica to the office. Numerous prototypes were already being sold in the market, publishing houses were going on-line, and you could already download an increasing number of reading materials from the Internet.

New forms of reading were only one aspect of the new digital revolution. In a few years, your car would drive itself to your programmed destination, changing routes if its info feed were to indicate traffic along the way. You might even be able to talk to your car as you drive, telling it to turn on the AC, turn down the volume on the CD player, read your E-mails. The walls in your house would contain picture frames that sense who is nearby and display that person's own pre-selected paintings: the Mona Lisa, Sunflowers, Campbell Soup Cans. Different people would see different artworks—their own selections—when they walk by the frames. All brought to you by Cybronics, of course. To make your life worth living.

I thought about Blade Runner and The Terminator and wondered whether I'd have been happier if I had been born in Italy during the Renaissance instead. Or maybe England during the Industrial Revolution or Chicago during the Depression. It was enough to make me think I wanted the airline liquor, but I barely touched my warm $4 mini-bottle of Scotch and stared out the window as the neat rows of brown and gray Queens houses lining the approach to the airport grew from Monopoly-size to doll-size to life-size.

When I got home, I called Lucille to check in and ask if by any chance she had heard from Schuyler. She hadn't, but now she knew he was missing. I told her I planned to take a few sick days. I tried to downplay it, but she knew me too well. And Lucille liked to earn her salary.

"Mr. Lightman, I hate to jump the gun, and I don't want to make you nervous, but I think we should hire that investigative service right away. The one run by your old friend."

"Bart Casey? You mean ISI?—"

"Yeah, ISI. The one we used that time—"

"Great idea," I said.

"Maybe they can find out whether Schuyler's used a credit card anywhere within the past couple of days. If you think that would help, Mr. Lightman."

This was a good idea, and Lucille had many of them. But twenty years as my secretary and she still called me "Mr. Lightman."

"I'll give Bart a call."

"I have his private number right here, Mr. Lightman."

I dialed and got my minor league nemesis on the third ring.

"How's the ol' back, Casey?" The same way I always led off with him.

"If not for you, Cliff my man, by now I'd probably be an over-the-hill benchwarmer with a .220 average and 18 RBI's and not enough dough to buy from the top shelf."

"One wild pitch and you went out and got a real job. Got rich to boot. So you admit I'm behind your success?"

"One monster pitch and I got me an insurance settlement big enough to open my shop. But thirty-odd years ain't healed my back yet. So how may I be of service today, my man?"

"It's serious, Casey. My son Schuyler is missing."

"That kid probably figured a way to fly into space or something, don't you think? Or get himself invisible?"

"Last time I saw him was the day before yesterday, in Portland. Working for Avery Kord and the Cybronics Corporation. Designing software. One minute he's in his apartment, the next a goon named Hank Driver's in his bed, beating the headlights out of a woman named Tammy Wood. And I think Driver may have had something to do with a murder. Kord's original partner, Justin Webb. Sky thought so, anyway."

"You don't say. Your kid had to go all the way out to Oregon to get jammed up with creeps?" He made a kind of double clicking "too bad" sound with his tongue. "I can call your office for his social and the detail stuff?"

"Lucille's probably waiting breathlessly by the phone."

"Actually, she's on my other line, Cliff."

"Give her a shout if you come up with anything. I may be tough to reach, Casey."

"That was some hard fucking fastball you had, my man. Too bad you couldn't put it over the plate."

It felt good to be doing something constructive, but I needed the help and support I had come home to get. I sat down in front of the monitor and double-clicked the mouse to get started.

When I finally managed to get the Mom.ava program on-line, Eliza looked harried. For an electronic avatar, anyway. Hair noticeably disheveled, makeup a bit smudged. Sky hadn't neglected a detail.

"Not what you'd think, Cliff," she said, the slight trepidation an accurate reproduction. She was the concerned Mom I remembered.

"Slow down, Lize, you're losing me."

"Must be my sizable RAM, makes me think too fast." The optical readers perched on top of the monitor watched me, a pair of eyes I had trouble becoming accustomed to. "Cybronics makes some pretty snazzy cryptography software," she said. "I've interpreted the code. I've read through the Lightman files. There's a personnel file, salary history, hire date, that sort of thing. Sky's resume. All innocuous. As well as a file labeled 'termination.' That's the scary one."

"You're not saying—"

"My guess is that it's used in the employment sense, Cliff," she said. "You know, if you quit or get fired, you're marked 'terminated.'" She sounded reassuring, but I could read the pain in her face. She seemed to avert her eyes and look down. I rubbed my own forehead and realized how sweaty I was. She twirled the front of her wiry brown hair in her fingers.

"Even the code-breaking program couldn't get through the encryption on that file. Avery Kord wrote the termination file himself, and he did a damn good job of scrambling it so it's impossible to decipher."

"Look, Lize," I said. "Kord wants to finish this subliminal suggestion software. Even if Katie completed it, I don't think she gave him the code. So I think he needs Sky."

"Until it's finished, anyway."

"Right."

"At which point, Kord isn't going to want Sky around anymore."

She shook her head. "I don't know, Cliff. The man recognizes Sky's a genius. Why not keep him designing profitable programs for the next forty years?"

"Because he knows too much, Lize. Especially about this program. And other things too."

Eliza nodded. "I'm just learning the ropes and can get around the system without too much difficulty. If Sky's half as smart as we think he is, and curious, he's already learned the ins and outs. And if that program works, hell, Kord will be able to use it to sell anything, do anything. Control anyone. Have the public eating off of his palmtop."

"I doubt that would sit too well with Congress or the Attorney General. But still, Lize, Sky seems so...irreplaceable."

"He's our son, Cliff. But he's also the best potential star witness for the prosecution. He can ruin Kord in the Congressional hearings. Look what the Clinton government put Microsoft through, and that was nothing compared to what's going on at Cybronics. So Sky's his worst nightmare. He knows which closets the skeletons are in. And I'll bet there are lots of them." My wife knitted her brow into the little ridged highways I remembered behind the top of her Canon as she tinkered with the shutter and aperture settings.

"There was Katie Wilnot."

"Another potential star witness who can bring the company down with her knowledge of the subliminal suggestion program."

"How do you know?"

"She and Sky were handpicked, Cliff. They tested out at the highest two IQ's at Cybronics. I've seen the files. I can only guess what happened to her."

"She's in a coma, Lize. She tried to kill herself. I don't know if some perverse test of the program caused her to do it or if she just couldn't deal with all the pressure he put her under. I heard her say she tried subliminal suggestion on a bunch of people at a seminar she taught in California. Implanted some kind of prototype of the program in their laptop computers to see if she could persuade them to change their negative opinions about Cybronics. She wanted to survey them in a few months. But Kord said that wasn't strong enough, he needed a more serious test."

"A life."

I nodded slowly. "Now Katie's 99 percent sure not to recover."

"That's one percent too much risk for Kord, Cliff. Trust me. At some point he's going to make his odds 100 percent."

I felt lightheaded and my heart hammered against my chest as I thought about the implications. I don't know how much time went by before I spoke again.

"Lize, I don't even know where Sky is. He's missing. The last time I was in his apartment, a guy named Hank was there. Henry Driver. Sky thought he was a suspect in the Justin Webb murder. When Kord found out that Sky was hacking around looking for more information, he went bonkers. I'm scared maybe Driver somehow found out what Sky was doing."

She stared at me, silent and as still as the day I was called in to identify her remains. Computer images don't breathe, I realized. You can't put your hand on the chest or your finger in front of the nose praying for the warmth of a breath, the way I did that day until the mortician pulled me away and let me wet his shoulder with my tears. For a moment, I wondered whether the screen had frozen. I tapped it lightly. The visual sensors above the monitor moved slightly and she nodded, blinked, chewed her lip.

"Just thinking, Cliff," she said.

"We don't have much to go on."

"Well, what clues do we have?"

"Cybronics has a few hundred locations."

"Not enough time to go to all of them." Her voice was edged with tension.

"There's Katie down in Tampa."

"I doubt he'd put Sky in the same location as Katie. Too risky."

"Well, there's that group Sky kept meeting with downtown. Katie was part of it. But I don't know anything about the others."

"Nothing?"

"Just that they rented a church basement. But the priests didn't know their names. Even Schuyler knows only their Net names. Some kind of secrecy thing."

"That's it?"

"They drank a few bottles of wine, Lize," I said.

"From France?"

I stared at the screen a bit before answering. Her eyes widened.

"Actually, from the Hudson Valley, Lize. Five Fingers Winery. I have a bottle of it."

Her eyes crinkled as she smiled. "Is it a nice day for a drive?"

I nodded.

"Hey," Eliza winked. "I have a lot of housework to do anyway. Just keep me posted." She was the woman I remembered, the positive, decisive one with a game plan. We had a problem, but we were going to take action. It was better than sitting on our hands.

"I wish I could touch you, Lize," I said, old emotions stirring out of hibernation. "I wish you were here to hold me."

"Close your eyes."

We were quiet for awhile as I moved into a dream, or a state that reminded me of one. My horror and trepidation about Kord and his plans for my son melted like hot liquid into a swirl of wonder and amazement at how real Eliza's animated reincarnation had become. I didn't feel silly at all as I closed my eyes, then opened them to see if hers were closed. They were. I quickly shut mine again, not wanting her to catch me cheating.

There were no fingers on the back of my neck, no arms around my shoulders, no fragrance of Chanel No. 5 sensualizing the air. Yet I felt calmer and reassured, recalling the warm feelings of her soft breasts and firm belly as they pressed flat against me through the texture of a knit cotton cardigan.

When I opened my eyes the cardigan was draped over her shoulders, and I wondered how she could have been programmed so accurately as to know which article of clothing I'd imagine her wearing. It had to be coincidence. But for an instant I was myself again, and she was Eliza in the flesh and blood.

"We're going to find him," she said, her tone serious.

I tried hard to smile. A lifetime of images of our son quickly began to scroll through my consciousness, paused frames on a VCR tape, a sobering pinch that woke me out of my hypnotic state. Superman lunch boxes and brown paper book covers and skinned knees and sunburns and tying up a baseball glove with oil in the pocket to break it in; a wrist broken in a fall from the top of the monkey bars; Eliza scrambling to make pancakes early enough to get him to school before the bell; winning science fair projects I never understood; a trio of fishing poles all being tugged at the same time: Sky's by a bluefish, mine by some seaweed and Eliza's by some unknown creature that snapped her line.

"No question, Cliff," she said, the confidence in her words betrayed by the worry in her tight expression. "We're his parents." The monitor's background had changed into a night scene, a starry blue sky, and Eliza shrunk into a small distant figure. She looked around in what appeared to be true amazement.

"There is a God, Cliff," she announced in a firm voice, with more certainty on the subject than I recalled either of us ever having.

I stared into the screen, allowing my eyes to unfocus they way they do when you look at those hidden 3-D image books, permitting myself to imagine I was walking under true starlight, her hand in mine. If there was a God, he was teasing me.

"We'll find Schuyler," she repeated.

She winked, and the display went blank and white as snow.

CHAPTER 24

"The name's Eno," the man behind the old wooden counter said, puka-shelled, tie-dyed, bell bottomed, looking eerily like the Sonny Bono tour guide at Cybronics and sounding like an old misplayed violin. A bright acrylic portrait of him smoking a fat cigar on a tropical beach hung on the wall behind him, doubling the psychedelic 1960's effect. It seemed incongruous in a dusty room composed of old random-width pine plank floors, an oak mantel, a couple of ancient wine barrels, and row after row of wooden shelves lined with wine bottles. "If you like a dry white, can I interest you in a taste of our best estate Riesling?"

"I'm not here to taste the wine, Mister Eno," I said, immediately on guard, wondering whether he was another copy of the Cybronics tour guide robot.

"Eno's the first name. Eno Loggia. But Eno's enough, so to speak. And 'scuse me for asking, but why come to a winery if not to taste the wine?"

I could see his point.

"I'm a private investigator, Eno." It felt only partly like a lie. I decided to use an investigative-sounding name rather than my own, just to be safe. "The name's Clay Blacker." I opened my wallet and quickly flipped it shut, as if he should have seen a badge or a license or whatever it is a P.I.'s supposed to carry.

"First investigator I ever met who didn't want to sniff the ol' bouquet, Blacker."

"I'm on the wagon."

"Too bad. A glass a day's good for the heart."

"It's the psyche I'm worried about."

"Well, we got some nice wine jellies, too. Help yourself on the way out." He pointed to a row of shelves lined with small glass jars filled with yellow and honey and deep red jellies with handwritten labels like Chardonnay and Merlot.

"I always thought jelly just came in flavors like grape and strawberry." The musty odor of all the old wood seemed to blend into the sweet smell of fermenting grapes. I breathed deeply, tried to relax. I waited until a customer left, so Eno and I were the only people in the room. A fan whirred faintly from somewhere out of eyeshot. A large oak table surrounded by old wooden chairs was littered with half-open wine bottles, unpacked crackers and a cheddar cheese bar on a board with a slicer sticking out of it. I pulled over one of the chairs and sat across the counter from where Eno stood.

"So what can I do for you?" he asked, his eye contact direct, his eyes seeming too wet to be Animatronic likenesses.

I pulled two pictures of Schuyler from my shirt pocket. Eliza had taken the first, up at Yale, and she somehow managed to capture a naivete in my son's face that you'd never believe if you had seen his resume or knew his IQ. The second was a wallet-size black-and-white that had that cold quality of a mug shot or a passport photo.

I stared at Eno's hands as he took the pictures from me. Perfect blue veins lined their backs, which were hairless and a bit pudgy for a thin guy. I wondered whether they housed electronic and mechanical devices that made them move. He had a Band-Aid on the back of one.

He glanced at the photos and shook his head.

"Never seen the guy," he said, handing them back. "What's his name?"

"Schuyler Lightman. He's missing."

Eno shrugged his shoulders. "You want to go out and see the grapes?"

"What the heck."

"Come on."

The pine planks creaked as we walked to the door. When we got outside he closed it behind us, locked it with a key and wrote "15" in chalk on a little blackboard on the door that now read:

HOLD YOUR HORSES. WE WILL BE BACK IN 15 MINUTES.

"We usually show the place by wagon," he said, tilting his head toward an old wooden carriage with a big old horse eating grass in front of it. "We get 50,000 visitors a year. But you can see more on foot."

I followed him along the rows and rows of vines that snaked around tall wooden stakes, red and green grapes of various varieties clustered on most. I listened to him tout the temperate climate and nutrient-rich soil of

MIND GAMES

the Hudson Valley. But what I noticed most in the ancient-looking vineyard was the little, almost inconspicuous LED display on the ground at the end of each row, red numerals barely showing from dirt-covered little black boxes half the size of the electrical outlets on your wall.

"What're these?" I asked, pointing at one of the boxes.

"Ah, the miracles of computer science."

"In a vineyard?"

Eno smiled. "These are attached to a central computer that contains all the codes that track how old the vines are, what the temperature's been throughout their lives, the rainfall and precipitation, soil moisture, and other factors. Some kind of formula then tells us the optimal time to pick and crush the grapes."

"A computer tells you that?"

"We got it for free, Mister Blacker."

"From where?"

"From some guys that wanted to test out their winemaking software. So they could work out the bugs and then begin selling it to vineyards. Ben and Jerry, I think they said were their names. They looked more like Mutt and Jeff. Little guy had hair like a porcupine. Anyway, we let them try it up here for free, and they left the prototype behind. Huge computer, I gotta tell you. Takes up too much space. I use it mostly for inventory purposes, to keep track of customers. Mailing lists. Scheduling, like when we last manured the place. It can also do real sophisticated stuff like run the pressers, monitor the temperature in the fermenting tanks, measure the chlorophyll content of the grapes to tell me when they're ripe. But I try not to overuse it. When it comes to the wine it wants to make, to tell you the truth—" he lowered his voice as if he didn't want the computer to hear—"we don't always do what the software tells us to do. Sometimes the old nose and taste buds work better. You've never seen a drunk computer, I bet."

"Where'd these two guys come from?"

"Somewhere in the northwest, I think. Used to wear these white running suits all the time. Funny thing, 'cause the most exercise they ever got was lifting their smelly cigars to their mouths. They hung out up here a couple a months, installing the equipment and testing it out. Maybe three years ago. Came back a year later to taste the wine they had programmed us to pick. One of 'em was an artist, too. Took a lot of pictures, some video. Drew a lot more. Of the place. Still lifes, bunches of grapes and stuff. And painted one of me."

"The one on the wall in your office?"

"If you call that an office." He nodded. "The guy made a lot of others of me, too. It was weird, how I'd be talking to him and he'd always have a sketch pad out. Made it hard to converse. It ain't exactly like I'm Tom Cruise or Paul Newman or anything."

"You have the pictures?"

"Nah. Just the painting. They took the others with them. Said they were to remember me by. Actually, they asked for permission to use my likeness as a model of some kind."

"You said okay?"

"Hey, I'll take my fifteen minutes any way I can get it. Life's too short to worry about it."

"What company were they with?"

"Cyber something, I think they said."

"Cybronics?"

He curled his lips. "Something like that. Their jackets had a big letter 'C' on the back, now that I think about it."

"That's where Schuyler Lightman used to work."

"The kid in the photographs?"

I nodded.

"So you made some progress, Mister Blacker."

"I wish. Can I see the central computer?"

We walked back to the office. The horse was still in the same place, still bent down and eating grass. As Eno fumbled with the key I asked what he had done to his hand.

"Sharp glass," he said. "If you ever break a wine bottle, be real careful when you pick up the pieces."

Once inside, he opened a door behind the counter and I followed him to a white personal computer. "That's just a small part of what they built here," he said, pointing behind him with an outstretched thumb like a hitchhiker. My eyes traced his thumbline to a white electronic machine that looked about the size of a double refrigerator. It had glass doors with a lock on them.

"I don't even have a key to it," Eno said. "Can't imagine what I'll do if it breaks. Of course, I'm not sure I'd know, given I don't even know exactly what it does."

He focused back on the personal computer keyboard and hit "Enter." A spreadsheet appeared on the screen. Its headings listed types of grapes, locations where planted, various temperature and moisture readings, and some dates.

"That's it?" I asked, expecting something more elaborate.

"Yup."

"Is there a title page or something?"

He moved the mouse and clicked.

VINEYARD OPTIMIZER 3.0 appeared, followed by a Cybronics logo.

"The guy who painted you," I asked, "when's the last time he came in here?"

"Jerry? Maybe a year ago."

We walked back out to the main room. I looked at the painting. The paint was too bright, like one of those cheap things you can buy at all too many art festivals on the street. But Eno's face and body had a realistic quality to them, an exactness that made them seem almost like a photograph. Probably done with the help of computer imaging or something, I thought.

I stared at the painting.

It took me a few seconds, but I realized what the problem was.

"If he painted the portrait up here at the vineyard, why palm trees and sand rather than grapevines and horse-drawn wagons?"

Eno smiled, the whiteness of his teeth contrasting against his dark mustache. He handed me a bottle of alcohol-free Merlot and a small jar of Chardonnay jelly.

"He had already painted the background, he told me. Before he got here, down in Tampa. Come to think of it, that's where he got his stinky cigars."

I glanced up at the painting again.

"Don't you smoke 'em?" I asked. "Like in the portrait?"

He shook his head from side to side. "Guess they took some artistic license." He smiled and his teeth sparkled. "Smoke's no good for either the crop or the taste buds. The only two things of any importance around here."

I began to reach for my wallet.

"They're on the house," he said, looking at the gifts he had given me.

"Thanks a lot," I said.

"Hey wait, Blacker" he said, walking back over to the terminal. "I gotta put you on our mailing list. I know you're on the wagon, so I'll try not to tempt you." He clicked the mouse a few times, then asked for my address.

As I answered, I realized I liked the guy. "My real name's Clifford Lightman," I said, embarrassed about having made one up. "It's my son I'm looking for."

"Sorry," he said, obviously correcting his input and adding the address I gave him. "I kind of thought the kid looks like you. That's L-I-G-H-T-M-A-N, right?"

I nodded.

"I'll let you know if anything turns up, Lightman."

I smiled as Eno licked a teaspoonful of Chardonnay jelly he took from an open jar.

CHAPTER 25

"We're going to Florida, Eliza," I said. "Tampa."

"You struck out at the winery?"

"Not completely."

"Why don't I wait up here?"

"Because I want you to come along."

"In that case, I'm already packed." She nodded. "Too bad you can't just download me to a laptop."

"Or to my lap. But for now, I'm afraid you'll have to sweat the cargo compartment."

The computer wasn't too difficult to disassemble or pack up, and I shipped it on ahead so she'd be at the Riverside Hotel before I got there. I wondered whether the concierge and bellhops would think I was nuts setting up a full-size PC in my room. I doubted they'd buy the story that it had special medical applications that I planned to employ over at Tampa Bay Memorial Hospital. I also doubted they'd ask for a refund of the 30 percent discount they offered me for being there on a hospital-affiliated trip.

Tampa was hot and humid. The Riverside Hotel was located right on the Bay, which was long and winding like a canal. It was a prime rowing location, and there were college crew teams assembling in the hotel lobby, sweaty and barely dressed. The men were tan, with biceps and pects that seemed glued on. And why did these muscular types always seem to lack moles and chest hair? The women were, well, I tried not to stare, knowing that Eliza wasn't too far away, but even she would have forgiven me. Sometimes testosterone controls involuntary muscles that guide eye movement, I learned long ago. Still, there was no need to tell Eliza. She looked better than they did anyway.

There was no listing for Cybronics in the phone book, so I decided to visit Katie. Tampa Bay Memorial was a short ride away, on a little island over a bridge. The hotel had a shuttle bus—outpatients and their families often stayed there—and my sense of direction wasn't great anyway, so I took it.

The only other passenger was a hospital patient scheduled to have his transplanted heart tested for rejection.

"It's my annual 12,000 mile check-up," Harry Cardinsky announced, extending his hand as he told me his name. "Got this heart 9 or 10 years ago. Soon my extended warranty expires."

"Really? A new heart?"

He nodded and smiled, which made his spotted leathery skin crease up around the eyes as if it were too big a size for his facial bones.

"I was out of it, Mister," he said. "The cardiologist in Miami told me I had played my last hand, it was time to cash in. A matter of days at most. But these doctors at Tampa Bay Memorial, they're miracle workers. This place has all the latest technology. A program that matches the ideal donor to the ideal donee. Or if you need open heart surgery, like a bypass, they can fix you up from another room using robotic hands, catheters and a monitor, without even having to open you up. They never give up around here, so you don't either. One day I'm knocking on heaven's door. Two weeks later I'm sipping a Tom Collins in Acapulco."

"You feel good?"

"Jog four miles a day. Only one other teenage organ I wish I had." He bent a bony forefinger so it appeared to hang limp.

By the time we arrived, I knew all about Harry's two daughters. Cindy was married to a struggling good-for-nothing podiatrist, and Mindy almost married a good-looking lawyer but ended up with a tubby guy who owned a fried chicken franchise in a flea market near Boca. Mindy's daughter almost lost a toe in a freak accident, but they managed to sew it back on and she was doing just fine, all things considered, except that Cindy's podiatrist husband refused to examine it because she was a relative.

I wished him luck, which he said he didn't need but would accept—the same way he'd always read the fortunes after eating Chinese food, even though he hated the cookies—and he wished me the best and expressed sympathy for my poor niece Katherine who I called Katie.

Okay, so I wasn't quite square with him. I had just met the guy.

Behind the area marked Reception and a receptionist who looked like George Foreman in army fatigues, there was a wall of plaques—arranged like the leaves on a tree—naming the hospital's biggest benefactors. Although all the plaques were in the same nondescript shade of copper, they were grouped into ranks of benefactors: so-called Platinum, Gold, Silver and Bronze. Like credit cards. I couldn't help staring at the biggest plaque, the one on top of the tree, although it didn't surprise me; it said, simply,

AVERY KORD AND FAMILY

The receptionist told me in his baritone voice that Katie Wilnot was in a private room up on the seventh floor. Turned out it was down a tiled corridor past a nurse's station and several other comatose, unconscious or seriously-ill neurological patients.

Nobody asked any questions. I guess they figured that if you were visiting someone on that particular corridor, you probably weren't there to do any harm. In fact, you probably couldn't make anybody worse, even with a gun.

It didn't surprise me that she had a plastic ventilator tube inserted through her trachea or that she was hooked up to a heart monitor, an automatic blood pressure cuff, and several intravenous drip units hanging on a metal pole. Her throat and her arm were black and blue and crusted with blood around the insertion points of the various devices. Her head was slightly elevated, propped up on a pillow. Her jaw was clenched. Above her were monitors that graphed out her heart rate, temperature and blood pressure. I thought another one mapped out her brain waves, too; I traced its wires to electrodes bandaged onto her shaved skull. Yet even the electrodes seemed par for the course. The brain waves on that monitor were shallow, forming little more than a straight line, in stark contrast to what appeared to be the vigorous beating of her heart.

The intravenous lines were threaded through a computerized pump hooked onto the middle of the I.V. pole, and the whole apparatus stood between Katie's bed and the window. If she could get up and open her eyes, she'd probably complain about how it blocked her view of Tampa Bay against the sunny horizon. I craned my neck a bit and watched the crew teams row past a television broadcasting station, past a Romanesque building that resembled a mosque, under a footbridge and right by the

Tampa Rey cigar factory's imposing neon sign and three monstrous oval smoke rings that hovered above a tractor-trailer sized Corona.

I pulled up a plastic chair and sat next to Katie, took her hand. It felt clammy, its fingers stiffer than I expected, not giving way as I pressed them. Her nails were polished red, and for some reason I didn't expect them to be so neatly trimmed.

"What can you tell me, Katie?" I asked, knowing there would be no reply. "What happened?" Her breaths were regular, routine, her chest moving up and down at a pace controlled electronically by the ventilator. "What did that bastard Avery Kord do to you?"

For a second I thought I saw her eyes twitch, maybe roll a bit under her heavy eyelids, the kind of movement I remember Sky's eyes making when I'd try to wake him for school and he wanted a few extra minutes of sleep. I quickly glanced at the brain wave monitor and thought a single wave jumped a bit higher than the rest.

Had to be my imagination, I knew. I mentioned Kord again while staring at the monitor. The waves stayed uniform.

I didn't hold her hand long before I started to think this was pointless. What could I learn about my son's whereabouts from a girl in a coma? I felt guilty for wasting time, for bopping around playing P.I. when I probably should have remained out in Portland. Yet I knew Eno's visitors spent a lot of time in Tampa, I knew Katie had tried to commit suicide down there, and I figured she might be the source of some clues.

I don't know what motivated me to kiss her on the forehead, but I did. There was no recognition, no flash of consciousness. Not even a flit of the eyelids.

I closed the door. I knew I had to be fast so I wouldn't get caught. The P.I. business wasn't really my thing. But my son's life was at stake, and maybe this young woman's, too. I opened her nightstand drawer and found a small black purse. A few quarters—perhaps the orderlies had already gotten to the dollar bills. No phone book, either. I tore past a tube of lipstick, a tampon, some keys—including a plastic card key—on a Donald Duck key ring. A compact mirror. A Cybronics business card, but the office address was the central facility in Portland. A driver's license showing her mother's address in Orlando. Another tube of lipstick, some eye liner. A folded copy of a Congressional subpoena requiring her to testify about Cybronics. And an acrylic tube containing a Tampa Rey Corona cigar.

I figured Sam Spade would have read the subpoena and pocketed the keys. So I read the subpoena and pocketed the keys. Then I quickly closed the purse and the drawer. My instincts were good. My hand was barely off the steel handle when a nurse walked in to check on Katie.

"You are a relative?" The heavy black woman in white eyed me suspiciously, a hint of Jamaica in her speech.

I nodded.

"She's not gettin' better," Charlene said, her name tag making the introduction. "It's a shame."

"Where did this happen?" I asked.

"Don't know. She don't talk, you know."

"But doctors and nurses do. What do people say?"

"They hope she go to a better place soon. Although she not suffering, I don't think. But you never can give up the hope, you know."

"Annie come here to visit?"

"Her mother?" Charlene smiled and nodded. "Almost every day. She do her nails, wash her hair. She be here tomorrow morning sure as the sun come out. She love this girl a lot, Mister—?"

"You can just call me—" I extended my hand and paused a bit. "Clay. Clay Wilnot. I'm a distant uncle."

"Uncle back home mean mother's brother," Charlene said. "How distant can you be?"

"I haven't seen this part of my family in many years. But when I heard about Katie—"

"Blood be thicker than rum. You'll be back tomorrow, I'm sure."

"I plan to be."

"Well, maybe her uncle be the miracle she need. She need to be remind of her childhood. That how she gonna wake up." Charlene smiled. "I seen that happen before, although nobody believe me." She took Katie's pulse at the wrist, glancing at her watch even though a monitor was checking it continuously and automatically.

She perceived my curiosity.

"Sometime the fancy machine read wrong," she explained. "The American doctors, they love the machine. They think because it's a machine, it's gotta be right. They think she just the living dead anyway. But me, I try to be a real nurse. Even though I just arrive, not too long ago."

"Thanks for trying." I smiled and walked out.

"That be your uncle Clay," I heard her telling Katie after I had gone through the doorway. "He love you and come a long way to see you after all these many years. He love you and he love your mother. Now you gonna come out of it and give him a big hug, like I know you can?"

There was no response, and I swallowed hard as I walked down the corridor toward the exit.

I grabbed a tall coffee at Starbucks and sat on a wooden bench to gather my thoughts. A few of the crew teams rowed around in the bay, some over by the cigar factory. It had been years since I had a drag of a stogie, and I thought about getting one. Something about the earthy taste of the coffee fed my craving. I figured it was because coffee and tobacco grow in the same part of the world. I wished I had taken the Corona from Katie's bag. She wouldn't have missed it, that seemed certain.

CHAPTER 26

"I lied a little, Lize," I said, pouring a pre-mixed margarita from the mini-bar into a glass full of ice I had gotten from a machine down the hall. Something about the humid Tampa climate changed my liquor preference.

She smiled but her brow furrowed.

"I told a nurse I was Katie's uncle Clay," I said. "Just trying to be careful."

"Seems harmless enough."

"So what next? We sure aren't going to learn anything from Katie Wilnot."

"You never know, Cliff."

"This time, I know. Her brain waves are flat as a pancake."

"But as long as she's still alive, Cliff—" Her words hung in the air and I noticed a tear in her eye. My next sip of the margarita went down hard. As I placed the glass on a side table, my hand trembled and the ice made a tinkling sound against the glass.

"I never thought I'd lose you, Eliza. You don't know how guilty—"

"Fuh-gedd-aboudit," she said, dropping her voice into a deep impersonation of someone like Sammy the Bull or Vinny the Chin.

"But I can't, Lize. That night—if I had stopped you—"

It had been brewing inside me ever since. I rarely shared my continued feelings of guilt with anyone. Sometimes I hid them from myself, made believe the therapy had worked, tried to be a model for Schuyler. But when she was alive, there was nothing I would have held back, and now I desperately needed Eliza to talk to. I didn't want to become a Harry Cardinsky, spilling my guts to any stranger who sits next to me on a shuttle bus and isn't deaf.

"Cliff, nothing could have stopped me. Get it through your head. I gave birth to that kid, nursed him. Raised him. I was going up to Yale and that was that."

The margarita glass looked frosty and felt icier when I picked it back up. I guzzled the second half of the drink. The lime sourness made my lips tighten. I went back into the mini-bar and took out a chocolate bar.

"So now what, Eliza? I have Katie's keys, but they're nondescript. A Segal, a Standard. A Honda key. A plastic key card. On a ring with a Donald Duck ornament."

Eliza shot me a questioning look.

"I stole them from her purse, Lize."

"Katie won't miss them. What else was in there?"

"A subpoena. She was supposed to testify in Congress two days after—"

"There's part of the explanation," she nodded. "Anything else?"

"The usual. Lipstick, a tampon, a compact. Loose change."

I suddenly felt choked for air, as if I had gone on an expensive vacation to Paris and just realized I had neglected to visit the Eiffel Tower.

A genius and a beauty and a health nut, Katie's mother had called her.

"There was also a cigar, Lize," I blurted out. "A fat thing George Burns would have loved. And so would some guys from Cybronics who spent a lot of time up at Eno's winery."

Eliza smiled. "Maybe Katie told you something after all."

CHAPTER 27

There was a slot for a card key by a door on a small side street away from the bay. I tried Katie's flat plastic card key. I wasn't surprised when the lock popped crisply open. I walked through the entrance.

Most of the place looked like—well, not like a cigar factory. I hadn't ever seen one before, but I expected dirty floors and dark old Cuban men with stained fingers sitting around rolling tobacco. I wasn't quite prepared for clean white porcelain and stainless steel machines. They tidily measured out each cigar's filler, weighed the tobacco on a scale and lined it up in short parallel lines that moved down a conveyor belt until each was wrapped by mechanical hands into a brown leaf. Then they were rolled, banded and dropped into a counter for boxing. It was a less noisy process than I'd guess, full of smooth whooshes and whirs and hums rather than harsh claps and thumps, soothing in its repetitive, uniform quality. And the smell of unsmoked tobacco was sweet, pleasant, nothing like its burning second-hand pungency.

But the cigar manufacturing process wasn't nearly as much of a surprise as the scene in the little office a few yards to my left. The door was open and I could see in.

Harry Cardinsky sat in a chair opposite the desk, wearing one of those white nylon Cybronics jackets, fingering an unlit cigar and occasionally chomping on it. When it wasn't in his mouth, I could see that he smiled as he spoke, although even the calm electronic whir of the machines was enough sound to prevent me from hearing him.

Whatever he was saying, though, seemed less important than his audience. Behind the desk, leaning back in a high leather chair with his feet up, wearing brown Topsiders without socks, was none other than Avery Kord. His tortoise shell rims were just a shade lighter than Harry's cigar.

He, too, had a smile on his face as Harry talked. An old Apple Mac sat on the shelf behind him. It had apparently been gutted and made into a tropical aquarium filled with swordtails and mollies, neons and a small eel.

My heart pounded like a piston and my toes curled up in my shoes, but I decided to take a gamble. I walked toward the office.

Two uniformed guards appeared, seemingly out of nowhere, and blocked the door, arms folded on their chests. I didn't notice much about them other than their size, which was not small; their uniforms, which were cherry red rather than the ubiquitous law enforcement blue we all come to expect; and the big black automatic weapons that dangled from their belts and distinguished them, along with their lack of white beards, from Salvation Army Santas at Christmas.

"That's far enough, Mister," one of them said, his gun swinging. He was the one I started to think of as Tweedledum.

"Hey, he's okay," a loud voice said from inside the office. "He's a friend of mine visiting his niece."

"You have a good memory, Harry," I said, my pulse quieting down in my ears. The Red Sea parted and I walked in.

"It's the gingko pills." Harry didn't lose his crinkle-eyed smile. The other man stood and extended his hand for me to shake. I was surprised by its warmth; I had expected dry ice.

"Avery Kord," he said.

"I know."

"Have a seat, Mister—"

I paused, thinking: Bond, James Bond. "Lightman. Clifford Lightman." I looked for a hint of discomfort, recognition, recollection. But I got nothing. Warm hand, cool personality.

"Hey," Harry said to me. "I didn't even know your name."

"But Mister Kord does," I said, turning to the man behind the desk and swallowing the golf ball that had formed in my throat. "Don't you, sir?"

He pursed his lips. "Not really, Mister Lightman."

"What about my son, Schuyler? You know him? Sky Lightman?"

Kord smiled widely, a plastic smile I recognized as phony. Same toothy smile he wore on television.

He shifted in his seat and I knew I had landed a solid jab. I wondered how he'd cover.

"Of course I know Shuyler, Mister Lightman."

"You two want to be alone?" Harry asked. "I can take a tour."

"Nah, that's okay, Dad," Kord said.

I could barely comprehend what I just heard. I struggled to control the quavering of my voice.

"Dad? You mean—" I pointed at Harry, then Kord, then Harry again. "You two?"

"Cardinsky was too long," Kord said.

"But Harry, what about Cindy and Mindy, your daughters?"

"That's all true, Clifford," Harry said. "They're pains in the butt, if you really want to know. But I love them like daughters. Because they are. I can't think of too many other reasons."

"But you didn't even mention Avery Kord!"

"Hey, my son's a big success, so why talk about him? Then you wouldn't listen to me complain about the things that really bother me. You'd tune out. You'd want to know all about my son. His company. You'd wonder about all the stupid rumors. Ever since Avery became this major megillah, nobody wants to hear about Harry. And some people—not you, Clifford, but there are bad people out there—they might ask me for money. Or worse. Try to kidnap me. You think I can just share every personal thing with every guy I sit next to on a bus? We live in a crazy, confused world."

"But don't we, Dad." Kord got up and walked over to a small cube-style refrigerator. He removed a pre-packaged ice cream cone and asked if I wanted one. I declined. The fridge was filled with them.

"When my father had his heart surgery, I came down here to visit," Kord said between licks and bites of his cone. "I liked the area. We needed a place in the southeast anyway, so I bought this cigar factory. It was a losing business in a building that was way too big. At first I was going to reconfigure the whole thing, but then I decided to keep a little bit. The old sign and all that. Sort of a souvenir. So all the stuff you see, the cigar machinery, that's only on the first floor. The upper floors are booming with software designers, systems architects. Geeks of every color and nationality." He smiled and bit off the entire chocolate-coated head of the cone in a single bite.

"But nothing says Cybronics anywhere. It's not even in the Tampa phone book."

He chewed and slurped loudly for a minute before continuing. "It's kind of a secret factory, Mister Lightman. A lot of my top people come through here. Not locals, by and large. A few, but not many. We design some of the test software here, special projects. Star Wars missile defense systems. Foreign intelligence. Space flight software for NASA." He lowered his voice to a conspiratorial whisper. "I'm trusting you because of your son. Please don't advertise this location."

"I don't plan to," I said. It was true. I just wanted my son back. "So you say you know Schuyler."

"How could I not?" He unraveled the paper from the cone, then bit the bottom and sucked leaking ice cream out of the hole he had made. His hands started getting messy, so he tossed a few cone crumbs into the fish tank and the rest into a metal garbage can. The eel was too busy swallowing one of the neons to notice.

"Sky and I interface almost every day in Portland. He's been one of my top employees since he joined us." Kord turned to his father. "Mr. Lightman's kid is one of the smartest people on the planet, Dad. He's way out on the right side of the bell curve."

"But he's missing, Harry," I said. "I'm looking for him."

Kord nodded. "So are we, Mister Lightman," he said. "I was terribly upset when I was informed he disappeared."

"You were upset?" My voice rose despite my efforts to stay even-tempered.

Kord cut me off. "Apart from liking him, Mister Lightman, your son is worth a lot to me in the future. Needless to say, we're all a bit mercenary." The way he smiled at me made me feel like a cockroach.

"Good at the mercenary stuff, too," his father injected. Kord didn't laugh.

"So of course I'm upset," the richest man in the world continued. "And I guess you know Schuyler was scheduled to testify in Congress soon. On Monday, I think."

I nodded as if I did.

"One of the last witnesses before next month's big vote on our business practices. Sky's so smart and knowledgeable about the company, and so presentable, I figured he'd win the whole thing for us."

I looked right into his eyes. They didn't waver. But his voice snapped and crackled so much I wondered if it would pop.

He continued. "I've had Sky's picture and prints electronically broadcast on police web sites worldwide. In case anyone spots him. And I've had computerized target maps printed up and sent to the Portland Police to help them search."

I wanted to believe the man. Something about him was amiable, childlike. But I thought of how he threatened Katie just a few days before she turned up in a coma. And Scarlett's suspicions about Justin Webb rung in my head as well. Still, I wasn't really sure of the facts—or of anything.

"When I asked about my son out at Cybronics, Mister Kord, they said they never heard of him."

"You mean at our Portland campus? I got a message that you stopped by."

I nodded, thinking it was pretentious to call it a campus since it wasn't a school. "They checked the computer. No employee by that name."

"Right," Kord said. "They would say that. I ordered that all your son's files be deleted."

"Deleted—?"

"Security precaution," he said, not missing a beat. "Our safety net software detected a break-in. Someone—a hacker using a digital agent of some kind—got past the firewall and rummaged through your son's files."

"So you erased them?"

He nodded. "For several reasons, Mister Lightman. Primarily, for his own protection. Someone unknown may have wanted access to personal info about him. Maybe others would come looking for the same data. Addresses. Social security info. You name it. And you never know what their motives might be."

"Why would someone want that stuff?"

He shrugged his shoulders. "I can't explain why some people go bad, Mister Lightman, but my industry unfortunately seems to attract some of the worst. Geniuses sometimes have a vicious streak. Others get depressed, turn inward." He paused, looking for a response. I sat stone still. "Reason number two: to protect Cybronics. I'll give you a for-instance. There's this computer virus called a Trojan horse. It's like a land mine. Some have called it a logic bomb. It waits until you step on it, until you open a file that contains it. Then the virus spills out and corrupts all of your software. Erases files. Transfers or alters data. And it can spread. When we were just starting out, a logic bomb shut us down for two weeks. The hacker went to jail for a year or so, but set me back more than two million bucks. Nowadays, with more sophisticated programs, a good hacker could do a lot more damage. Could potentially close us for good. My doomsday scenario is some smart programmer who works for us goes postal, so to speak. Internal sabotage."

"But why would someone break into my son's files?" Now I was sweating. Cybronics had detected Eliza's moves, and I wondered how much else Kord knew.

"How well do you know your son, Mister Lightman?"

"How well?"

"I've been in this business a long time. I've seen a lot of these computer geeks get into cults and what have you. Some just go in for the crystals, the vortexes in Sedona, Arizona, that kind of stuff. But others take it further. Devil worshipping. The Jim Jones, Heaven's Gate, mass suicide kind of stuff. Scary stuff."

"So you're saying—" I immediately started to wonder about Sky's group meetings, about Schuyler's defensiveness when I asked about them.

Kord shook his head. "Not necessarily. But anything's possible. He was fooling around in the holography lab before this happened; who knows what kind of thing he was trying to create in there? And the security breach in his files occurred right after that. Just before he disappeared. I hate to think the worst." His tone of voice became reassuring in a way I found false and arrogant; yet he was telling me far more than I would have guessed if he really had something to hide.

I was tempted to say something about Katie Wilnot, about the subliminal suggestion program, anything to try to push the guy's buttons. But I knew I'd get nowhere. If he was being honest, it would be useless and insulting to bring up matters irrelevant to Schuyler. And if he was the calculating psychopath I believed him to be, it could further jeopardize my son's life. So I tried to keep a few cards close to the vest.

But he was too smart even for my thought-out silence.

"You're down here visiting your son's colleague Katie, no doubt."

"A tragedy," I said.

"A shame," he agreed. "God knows what the public will think."

"What do you mean?"

"She also had a subpoena. It's going to look awful that an employee who was about to testify—" He cut himself off and shifted to defense. "We employ 60,000 people, Mister Lightman. We're at the forefront of the Information Age. We have the luxury of choosing among the country's—the world's—best and brightest. So fortunately, the number of tragedies that befall us is a tiny percentage. We're on every top ten list of best companies to work for. Heck, I'm sure Schuyler's told you so as well. But she's a nice kid, that Katie. Smart beyond her years. One of my best. I hope she pulls through, but it's not the first time this kind of thing has happened. And I guess it won't be the last."

I wasn't sure I'd ever meet Kord again, so I decided I had to play one more card.

"Sky was pretty upset recently," I said.

"Yes?"

"Well, he kind of worships you, Mister Kord—" I tried to look sheepish—"and, well, he was devastated when you kind of yelled at him."

"I what?" His emphasis would have made his question seem genuine to someone who was uncertain about what had happened. But before I could respond, he seemed to remember.

"Oh, that," he said, almost to himself. "Your son has good motives. He was trying to help me, actually. But he was hacking. You know what that is?"

"I have a pretty good idea."

"It's like trespassing on somebody else's digital property. Invading their privacy. Seeing data they thought was private." He glanced over at his father, who tilted his head almost imperceptibly. "Can you imagine the kind of press we'd get if one of our top employees were implicated in something like that?"

"I thought young computer guys always do it," I said.

"Not at Cybronics, Mister Lightman. Next thing you know, the government would be saying we crack into our competitors' systems to keep them out of the market. We just can't tolerate it, as a matter of policy. I'm sure you understand."

I could, and I didn't know what to believe.

"I appreciate your help, Mister Kord," I said, rising slowly from my chair. "And I never thanked you in person for the financial support. It changed our lives. Put Sky through college. So thanks."

"Hey, Sky's the best darned software architect I ever had. So it is I who should be thanking you."

"Let's not get all silly now," Harry said, getting up and shaking my hand. "There's a lot more to life than just money. We have more money than most countries, Avery, and what good is it?"

"What do you mean, Dad?" Kord's voice cracked.

"Well, it didn't buy me a new heart when I needed one. I had to wait until the last minute like everybody else. It got so bad every time I passed a car wreck I prayed the driver had my blood type. One of them finally did, otherwise I'd be hamburger."

"Some things are beyond monetary reach, Dad," Kord said. "That's why I keep almost all of it in Cybronics stock." He looked at me. "Okay, I have about fifty million in real money. But the rest, what puts me number one on the Forbes list, is all my stock in the company. Keeps me loyal. We were up even when the market tanked. But if the company ever goes bust, I have to get a real job."

"About as much chance as the sun failing to rise," Harry said. "As much chance as Cindy and Mindy and their good-for-nothing husbands making me a happy old man."

"Come on, Dad. I have to fly out of here in a few more hours. Let's lighten up."

I wondered whether this was all too easy, whether they were hiding something. I asked for a look at the factory, fully expecting Kord to refuse my request. I was already planning a break-in after midnight.

"No problem at all," he said. "Dad, would you mind—"

"A tour? No problem at all," Harry echoed as I shook hands with his son.

We started on two and worked our way up, sometimes taking the stairs and sometimes the elevator. Except for Tampa Bay outside the windows, there was little to distinguish the glass-walled offices and glowing computer monitors and space-suited employees from those at the Cybronics facility in Portland.

"Be sure to watch 60 Minutes on Sunday," Harry said as we strolled past a series of glass-walled offices and gray workstations on the eleventh floor. "It will feature My Son The Rich Dork and his new fifty million dollar house. It's got all the latest technological stuff."

"Like computerized pictures on his walls that he can change at the push of a button? I think I've read about those."

"Pictures? He's got computerized walls, Clifford. So he can keep changing around the layout whenever he feels like it. Capture a burglar by building a prison right around him until the cops arrive. Not to mention building me a little live-in apartment in a corner, which he will be able to remove by pushing a button the day after I drop dead. I was there, so I know. Believe me. I have to shit, I push a button and a robot pushes a toilet under me. And wipes my behind when I'm done."

I looked at him with a brow I knew was knitted.

"That's not really true, is it?" I asked.

Harry chuckled. "No," he said. "Only the part where I said, 'I have to shit.'"

He stopped in the men's room and left me to roam around. Nothing seemed suspicious—although I wasn't sure what to look for. But the unconcerned freedom he allowed me made me think I wouldn't find anything in the place. They sure weren't afraid I'd find Schuyler here. While I waited, my gaze was drawn to a flat computer monitor just outside the men's room. Horizontal banners of stock prices, sports scores and weather data flowed across it hypnotically.

"You watch 60 Minutes this Sunday," Harry said, poking my shoulder to catch my attention when he rejoined me. "It's going to be interactive. That mean's he's going to send some kind of computer stuff to everybody with a computer and a modem. Kind of a present. A surprise. He may be the richest boy in the world, but I'm still proud of him. I think this time he's even going to tell the world who his father really is."

"He doesn't usually?"

Harry shook his head, resignation in his eyes.

"He was once just a little buck-toothed kid who needed braces and orthopedic shoes. There isn't anything in the world I wouldn't do for him, believe me. I was a big help to him when he got started. Gave him a big push. But now he always leaves me out of it. For my own protection, he tells me."

His reference to when Avery Kord got started was an opening I couldn't resist.

"Harry, what do you think about those old Justin Webb stories?"

He grinned as if he thought it a funny subject.

"Justin was a good friend of Avery's, Clifford. He used to come to our house for lunch when they were schoolboys. They played t-ball together, dissected frogs. Would have double-dated, if Avery could have gotten a date. Founded Cybronics together, with a little financial backing from Yours Truly. There's no way my son would have had anything to do with it."

"I read that Avery was on the radio that day. And was shocked when he found out."

"A talk show. I knew the host, I got him the slot. Cybronics was a little nothing back then, and so was my son. The show would be good publicity, I figured. Nobody had ever heard of Cybronics. Well, lots of people knew the company by the end of that day. Unfortunately, not because of the talk show."

"But why have all the rumors persisted?"

He shrugged his shoulders. "Because they never caught the guy that did it, that's why. Besides, what else are they going to talk about in Portland? The weather? It rains."

We finished touring the eleventh and twelfth floors. By the time we finished twelve, I wasn't in the mood for much more of Harry Cardinsky. The elevator showed that only thirteen and fourteen remained. He noticed me looking at the lit-up numbers.

"Just two more, Clifford," Harry said. "We still have to hit the unlucky number. Most buildings don't even have a thirteenth floor, but Avery's not superstitious."

"Seems to have worked for him," I replied. "You got a few four-leaf clovers around for me?"

"You'll find Sky." Harry smiled and nodded.

"Maybe. But not here." I decided to skip thirteen and pushed the button for fourteen. When the door opened, I peered out quickly without walking around. Then I stepped back in and pressed number one. I felt my stomach rise toward my neck as the elevator descended at an uncomfortable speed. "Let's call it a day."

"You sure, Clifford?" he asked, engaging me in a handshake that felt cool and reptilian. "You're such a good listener. And you understand fatherhood."

"I wish I did, Harry," I said. "Maybe I wouldn't have a missing son to go find."

CHAPTER 28

The pre-mixed margarita didn't help. Or the Dewar's. I tossed and turned so much that the sheet pulled free from the bed and was wrapped around my waist like a toga. I missed some of the ways Eliza used to help me relax. Her computer image didn't quite suffice. She again reminded me that the virtual reality headset and full-sensation bodysuit would be a trip to the past. She wanted it too, she said. I planned to buy them as soon as I had the chance. I didn't even know who sold that kind of stuff.

The immediate problem was, I didn't know what to believe about Schuyler's disappearance. Kord seemed unfazed by my visit to the factory. I dealt with stockbrokers and their complaining clients every day, and I thought I had the training and experience to recognize lying. Now I wasn't so sure. He had a rational explanation for the deleted files, he didn't hide his connection to Katie Wilnot or his argument with Schuyler, and he let me see the whole plant. He mentioned the subpoenas. I began to second-guess my instincts.

I took a quick morning shower. As I walked out of the bathroom past the room door I noticed that a complimentary USA Today had been slipped under it. A three-inch header caught my eye:

SIX DEAD IN APPARENT SUICIDE

The paper shook visibly in my hands as I read about three men and three women found dead out on Fisherman's Wharf in San Francisco. They all lay face up and wore t-shirts that read, "Whoever has the most things when he dies, wins." They had apparently mixed a lethal dose of cyanide into a gallon of Gatorade; a cracked glass pitcher was found nearby.

The group's identities were being withheld pending notification of their families. Preliminary reports suggested they all worked for high-tech companies. IBM. Intel. Cisco. I didn't see any reference to Cybronics. A color photograph of the scene showed them already covered up with a black tarp.

I turned on the TV, and as I flipped the channels I repeatedly saw images of seagulls gliding over the Golden Gate Bridge in the foggy orange-gray light of the San Francisco dawn.

A wave of nausea welled up inside me as I walked back into the bathroom and vomited a disgusting red-streaked acidic substance into the toilet. Was Schuyler one of the six? My skin was clammy and I felt strangely removed from my body, as if its thumping sweating tightening retching clawing reactions were happening to someone or something else.

There was a TV speaker in the bathroom. From a distance not far enough away, I heard something about a note found in the bottom of the Gatorade pitcher, initialed by all six of them. It said something to the effect that high technology companies and executives were being unfairly treated by Congress and the courts—Cybronics and Avery Kord in particular, as well as Microsoft—and that they wanted their deaths to call attention to the shortsighted inhumanity of those whose backward antitech thinking would send us all back to the Middle Ages. The commentators were pointing out that they were the antithesis of the Unabomber: he killed others to make some kind of warped statement against technology; they apparently killed themselves in a pro-tech frenzy.

I didn't calm down, but at some point my soul and my brain and my body reconvened in an effort to operate as a single being. I figured the San Francisco Six were probably some of the people in Katie's seminar, but I couldn't be sure. If all she planted in her prototype program were some pro-Cybronics messages, it sure was potent. Nor did I have any idea whether Sky was one of the six. I managed to call my office to ask Lucille whether anyone from San Francisco had contacted her. Through the telephone receiver, I could hear that she had on a television or a radio and was listening for the same news I was. Then I had her switch me over to my boss, so I could tell him I was taking an official leave of absence to find my son. He sent me back to Lucille, who had been placed on hold by the San Francisco sheriff's office. She patched me in. We listened to an unbearably repetitious Muzak version of "Up, Up and Away" before someone finally picked up. I explained who I was and why I was calling.

"We didn't call you?" the voice asked.

"No."

"Well, we're making the calls now. So if you get one, you'll know..."

"Why can't you just tell me? If I give you his name, and he's not in the group, you can just deny it."

"Different unit. Besides, how do I know you're who you say, and not a reporter? Or a suspect?"

"How could I be a suspect? It was a suicide!"

"That's what the papers say," came the reply. "But until the investigation is complete, that's just a prediction. If you catch my drift."

"Loud and clear," I said, but he hung up.

Then I instructed Lucille to get an atlas and call the police department in every city in the United States, from A to Z, tell them all about Schuyler and fax his photograph if they didn't have one.

"Got it," she said. "By the way, Mr. Lightman, I spoke to ISI. Sky hasn't used a credit card in a month. Mr. Casey said to tell you he struck out. But that other man you asked him about—that Driver guy—"

"Hank."

"Hank. Henry. Whatever. It turns out he's got a criminal record, Mr. Lightman. If you like, I can fax the ISI report to your room."

"I like."

As soon as I hung up, the fax started coming through.

It was a three-page report. It included a criminal history that reflected old convictions for loitering, unlicensed gun possession and trafficking in child pornography. Two other child porn arrests resulting in dropped charges. His credit history was ordinary, as were his deposits and withdrawals from a savings bank based in Portland. He had a safe deposit box, which I figured was probably a common necessity for people who need to stash child porn. But he also had an account at a bank in the Cayman Islands. I was curious about that; it didn't quite fit the picture. But other than the fact that it existed, there was no available information. A footnote to the report recited Cayman bank secrecy laws. There was a handwritten, oversized exclamation point next to the footnote.

CHAPTER 29

After a cup of black coffee in the lobby lounge and a free refill, I wandered a few blocks into the business district until I found a Radio Shack. I paced around waiting for it to open. The clerk must have thought I was nuts. Most rational people don't need to wait outside a store just to buy a cheap cassette player.

I took the shuttle bus to Tampa Bay Memorial. No Harry Cardinsky this morning. I was almost disappointed.

This was Florida, not too far from Orlando, and the hospital had a busy children's wing, so I wasn't surprised to find a few Disney tapes in the gift shop. I bought one called Sing-A-Long Songs. It featured the Seven Dwarves singing Hi-Ho, as well as Bear Necessities from the *Jungle Book* and some more recent *Aladdin* and *Lion King* numbers. I figured it would be as good as any. Heck, I was betting on a longshot.

Katie's mother was already in the room when I arrived. Katie's skin looked grayer, a sign I perceived as negative.

"Hello, Annie," I said, extending my hand.

Mrs. Wilnot looked at me but her expression was blank.

"She's really sick today," Annie said in a quiet voice. "Internal bleeding. She may need a transfusion."

"What's her blood type?"

"AB positive. The universal recipient."

"I'm O positive. I'd be happy to give mine." I smiled as I made the offer. "All the scotch and tequila in it might calm her down."

She allowed herself a slight smile.

"Why do you care about her?" she asked.

"My son's missing," I said. "As I told you, he designs software for Cybronics. I think maybe there's a connection."

She shook her head from side to side, looked at the floor. I did, too. The tile was old and cracking, free of dirt but stained with years of sickness, the rolling wheels of I.V. poles and gurneys and wheelchairs, the worn-out rubber soles of mournful visitors.

"I brought something with me," I announced to the room.

Annie glanced over as I opened the Radio Shack bag, took the cassette player out of the box and inserted the batteries. Then I struggled with the plastic jewel-box that held the cassette. I bent a corner back and forth repeatedly until my finger hurt and the plastic cracked open.

Two worried older adults and a comatose patient in a neuro ward are not your usual audience for Simba and Baloo and Ariel. Trust me, the theme songs and the pale green hospital room that smelled of stale urine were a strange combination.

Charlene walked in at the end of Timon and Pumba's rendition of Hakuna Matata, "means no worries," and smiled broadly, white teeth gleaming against her black skin. Her mouth would have made a great billboard for Colgate or Crest.

"I told you your Uncle Clay be coming back for you, honey," she said, holding Katie's hand as she took her pulse.

"A little fast this morning," Charlene said, looking up. "132. Like she just jog a few miles or have a high fever."

Charlene closed the translucent privacy curtain to take Katie's temperature and clean her up. I stood in the hallway and glanced down the hall as Pocahontas belted out some musical questions about whether you can paint with all the colors of the wind. I knew I couldn't.

"A child in there?" asked a stooped old lady shuffling along with the aid of a metal walker. At her pained pace, I estimated she'd reach the end of the corridor in a few hours.

"Not exactly," I said.

"Shame. At least I've lived my life."

"Hey, look!" Charlene yelled out. I rushed back inside. The curtain was open and so was the front of Katie's blue hospital gown.

"No time to be modest," Charlene explained. "Look at her eyes."

They were open. I leaned over to get a closer look. The pupils widened mildly as my head blocked the fluorescent light.

They suggested consciousness.

I glanced up at the brain wave monitor. I didn't know how to read it, but the map it graphed out went from tracing an almost straight line to outlining the Catskills. The monitor next to it showed a pulse of 145.

"Katie," her mother said.

"Sweetheart," whispered Charlene.

"Forget about your worries and your strife," bellowed Baloo and Mowgli.

There seemed to be some kind of glimmer in her eyes, a flicker, but still no physical response. No movement.

I took her hand.

"Katie, can you hear me? Katie, can you hear me? Katie?"

Still nothing.

"Katie, I'm Schuyler Lightman's father. Sky works with you at Cybronics. Do you understand?"

Her eyes looked wetter. I glanced at the lines on her monitors. The Catskills were looking more like the Himalayas. Her blood pressure cuff inflated automatically every five minutes. The latest readout was 200/120.

"That's high," Charlene said. "I'd better get a doctor."

Charlene walked out.

I sat next to Annie and gave her Katie's hand.

"Please, Katie, come back," she said. "Come on, Katie."

Side one of the cassette tape ran out. Annie started singing. Her voice was melodic, almost operatic, more mellifluous than anything on the Disney tape. But the words that came out were even a step farther removed from Mozart or Verdi or The Rolling Stones.

"FLINTSTONES, MEET THE FLINTSTONES, THEY'RE A MODERN STONE-AGE FAM - I - LEE - - -"

I would have pinched myself but I knew I was awake. My dreams were never this outrageous.

I talked to Katie, calmly, directly into her ear, softly but louder than a whisper, as her mother sang.

"Avery Kord," I said. "Saint Andrew's Church. I saw him on the computer screen."

"FROM THE TOWN OF BEDROCK—"

"Avery Kord caused this, didn't he, Katie?"

"THEY'RE A PAGE RIGHT OUT OF HIS - TO - REE!"

"Katie, Avery Kord did something bad, didn't he?"

Blood pressure 214/123. Pulse 148. Eyes open, conscious, but not responsive. Where the heck were Charlene and a doctor?

"Katie, let's try something. One blink for yes, two for no. Can you blink?"

A mild flit of the eyelids. Barely perceptible. Or was it my imagination? I wasn't certain.

"LET'S RIDE WITH THE FAMILY DOWN THE STREET"

"Katie, did Avery Kord do something bad?"

A definite blink, I thought.

"THROUGH THE COURTESY OF FRED'S TWO FEET—"

"Did he do something to you over in Orlando?"

"WHEN YOU'RE WITH THE FLINTSTONES, HAVE A YABBA-DABBA-DOO-TIME—"

A blink.

"A DABBA-DOO TIME—"

"Did he make you test the subliminal suggestion program?"

Another blink? Not clear.

"Did you finish creating the program?"

A flit? I wasn't sure.

"Is it finalized? Did you send Avery Kord the codes?"

Two blinks. I was certain. Or was it one? Annie Wilnot was looking, but her mind seemed far removed, somewhere in Hanna-Barbera land. I couldn't tell what she noticed. I wasn't sure what it all meant, but I suspected Kord still needed Sky to complete and perfect the program.

Blood pressure 226/130. Pulse 170. Still no nurse, no doctor.

"You tried to resist but couldn't?"

"WE'LL HAVE A GAY ALL TIME! WILLLLLLLMA!"

The heart rate monitor suddenly went flat and started beeping. The blood pressure monitor showed a steep drop. The brain waves lapsed back from tracing the Himalayas to sketching the edge of a sidewalk.

Charlene and a doctor wearing a green scrub suit and a surgical mask and cap finally walked into the room. The doctor glanced at the monitors just as they all started tracing straight lines and sounding out a chorus of whines. His deeply-lined eyes looked sad and tired and defeated.

The doctor ran out into the hall without removing his mask and yelled "defibrillator!" He continued down the hall and left the scene as two doctors in white lab coats and the machine took his place so quickly I thought they must have been sitting outside the room. But the doctors, assisted by Charlene and repeated mega-jolts of electrical charges, couldn't bring her back.

When it was over, Charlene closed Katie's eyes with her fingers. Tears filled her own, as they did mine. Annie was humming "Meet George Jetson." I was sure she hadn't noticed her daughter's blinks. Or forgot them if she had. Annie had moved into a cartoon universe in which brightly colored people and clothed animals jump off cliffs and lie down on train tracks and dive out of airplanes without parachutes, all ready to come back for the next segment or the next episode.

Katie had been conscious long enough to tantalize me, but I was the only one who'd ever know. And I wasn't sure.

As Charlene sat with Annie and stroked her hair, I picked up the cassette player and walked out of the room. The old lady with the walker still ambled down the corridor. She had gotten about ten yards farther.

"A shame," she said. "At least I've lived my life."

"You still are," I said, rushing by as I hit the rewind button.

I followed the signs and the yellow line along the wall until I reached the children's wing. I walked toward the nurse's station but as I passed a waiting room, I noticed seven or eight children gathered around a young woman reading *The Cat In The Hat.*

I walked in and sat down. The children all looked at me. One was in a wheelchair. Two had no hair.

"May I help you?" the woman asked.

"I just wanted to give you this little present," I said. I handed over the tape player. "It's for this wing."

"Thank you, sir," the woman said.

"Let's hear it," one of the children said, glancing at it.

"Yeah, let's play it."

The woman hit the play button. In short order, Baloo was crooning, "the bear necessities, the simple bear necessities, forget about your worries and your strife—"

The kid in the wheelchair smiled.

A few minutes later I walked out into a scorching, humid Florida afternoon. I needed Eliza and I needed a stiff drink and I needed a way to save my son before it was too late.

If it wasn't already.

CHAPTER 30

"Katie's dead," I said to Eliza. "Cardiac arrest."
"You sure that's the cause?"
"I was there."
"She had I.V. lines?"
"Right."
"Wires?"
"Electrodes. To measure brain activity."
"Oh?" Eliza asked. "Did you see whether the electricity was going in or out?"
"Of course not."
"So then you don't know, Cliff," she said.
"Come on, Lize."
"Cliff, when I was an insurance photographer, you wouldn't believe the kind of stuff I saw. A little 4-inch stick marked up as a 12-inch ruler, for example. So when a claimant photographed a pothole with the stick next to it, the hole looked three times bigger than it really was. Things aren't always what they appear, is what I'm saying."
"She's the seventh person in the computer industry to die under suspicious circumstances this week. Six in this cult thing. There was a note."
"My point exactly."
"You really think he'd—"
"Go that far? Who knows? But where's the line between murder and convincing someone to do it? You know subliminal suggestion is what they used to call brainwashing."
"So you think Sky's probably next?"
"Let's hope he's still next," she said. "Do we know he's not one of the six out in California?"

"Not for sure, although my guess is they were part of that seminar Katie was talking about. Maybe they overreacted or something. Hang on." I picked up the phone and dialed the hotel operator. Lucille had called to say there was still no word from San Francisco. I hung up and looked back at the monitor.

"No new info?" Eliza asked.

I shook my head.

"Kord's going to be on Sixty Minutes this week, too. If the San Francisco thing doesn't trump his guest appearance. He plans to show the world what a lovable guy he is. What great toys his company makes. If you have a computer, the bastard's even going to zap some kind of surprise present to you."

I stared at Eliza. I doubted the computer's optic sensors could pick up the anguish in my face, but I could see it in hers. She was ashen. It was hard to believe the monitor could reproduce such subtlety in shading.

"I never felt so lost, Eliza. Like I'm treading water somewhere out in the middle of the Atlantic. I look around and see nothing but water, miles and miles of water against a darkening sky. The sun is setting and my arms and legs are tiring out."

"Shut up," she blurted out. "I have a plan." Her voice was louder than I thought the speakers could go.

"Sorry, I just—"

"Slap yourself in the face for me." She cut me off at full steam. "At least until you get that virtual reality headset and the sensation suit. Then I'll be able to do it myself."

"But we don't even know where he is, Lize. Or if—"

"You work on finding him, Cliff. Phone calls. Scarlett. That cop in Portland. Your whole damn Rolodex. You put up posters. Ads in the paper. The whole shebang. As fast as humanly possible."

"Right," I nodded. "I already have Lucille making a zillion phone calls. Using Investigative Services International. But if we advertise that we're looking for a drop of olive oil in the North Sea, we'd probably find it faster than we'll find Sky."

"You can't win if you don't play," she said. "But that's just part one. Because while you're canvassing the country, I'm going to be loading up."

The optical sensors must have picked up the quizzical look on my face. She answered before I asked.

"Absorbing some data. I'm going to hack my way into the virus creation lab. The place where they concoct the latest, greatest computer cancers."

"To do what, Lize?"

She rubbed her forehead, twirled her hair. She was thinking and appeared uncomfortable.

"Look," she finally said. "Let's assume he's alive, okay? Unless and until we hear otherwise. Chances are he's somewhere out there, sitting in front of a computer, working on this subliminal suggestion project. Being forced to work on it. Maybe Kord plans to get rid of Sky when he's no longer useful, but for now Kord needs him to finish developing the program. We don't know anything for sure. But if we can interfere with Cybronics' systems—corrupt them, uninstall the subliminal suggestion program, delete it, erase it, ruin the operating system—then we can buy some time to locate Sky and get him out of there."

"But we don't have a clue where in the world he is, Eliza! What city, or even what country! And we don't know anything about the software he's working on! Its name. His password. We don't even know what name Sky himself uses to log on! His screen name could be one of those hacker names like Acid Rock or Heavy Metal. Or it could be Abraham Lincoln or Isaac Newton or Babe Ruth!"

"I know, Cliff," she said, her voice strangely calm. That's why we're going to have to destroy every single bit of the Cybronics system. Every program. Every code. Every signal. Every hard drive. Everywhere. Their systems will be so screwed up, they'll have a lot more to worry about than Schuyler Lightman. They might well decide they need Sky's brilliance and expertise to help get them out of their world-class jam. In other words, we have to do a lot of damage to save his ass. That's why I need state-of-the-art viruses."

I stared and wondered if her logic circuits had been tampered with. "What if he's finished the subliminal suggestion program and is a Guinea pig in some crazy kind of suicide test? How will we stop him if the program prompts him to—to go off and—"

"The program will never take effect, Cliff. Sky's computer will be nuked along with the rest."

"How on earth are we going to do all that?"

Eliza stared at me with an expression I knew too well. A facial cast I had repressed since I had last seen it on the day of a terrible Nor'easter.

It was a look that said she knew I'd disapprove, but that nothing in the universe—certainly nothing I might do—could stop her.

"I'm going to fill myself up like a Trojan horse with clones of the most devastating, most incurable fucking land-mine, Pandora's box computer viruses ever to exist," she said, her eyes narrowing into feline slits. "Then I'm going to spread a goddamned electronic AIDS virus through every single micron of Avery Kord's digital empire. The atomic bomb of logic viruses is going to explode like a series of plagues Avery Kord couldn't imagine in his wildest nightmares. By the time I'm through, Kord's central computer system's gonna think two plus two is an unsolvable conundrum."

I continued to stare at her. I don't know if I was in awe or disbelief.

"Eliza." I wasn't sure I knew what to say, but that didn't stop me from talking. "If you can get through some of the systems, won't some kind of defensive programs destroy you? And even if they don't, if you manage to do all you said, ruin all Cybronics' systems, wouldn't you end up destroying yourself in the process? I may be simpleminded, but the code that makes you work is part of the Cybronics system too. Sky created you out in Portland. You only come alive when the computer's plugged into a phone line, into the company's databases. Destroy those databases, and—"

"I have to do it, Cliff," she said, her voice firm. "If you can't find him physically, this is the only way."

"You didn't answer my question, Lize."

"I didn't want to."

I felt my muscles tense. I knew I was hyperventilating but I couldn't stop. A sharp pain stung me near my heart.

"I don't want to lose you again, Eliza," I managed to mouth.

"And I don't want to lose what we have either, Cliff," she responded, biting her lip. She looked as troubled as I felt. I wanted to hold her in my arms, to feel the beating of her heart, the breaths heaving in her chest. But I had to settle for memory and illusion. She was a damn good wife. And a world-class avatar.

"He's my son," she said, the resolve back in her tone. "You'll probably have to hit the Send button a few thousand times to distribute E-mails that contain the viruses. I haven't worked out the details yet."

"It's totally illegal," I called out. "Not that it matters." I had to raise my voice because I had walked away from the monitor and over to the mini-bar. I began to calculate what it would cost me to drink every miniature bottle of liquor in it. I was going to start with the Dewar's, the pre-mixed margaritas, the Remy Martin VSOP. After that there were two Tanquerays, a Bacardi, a couple of Johnny Walkers and some Chivas. A couple of Glenlivets, some Crown Royal, a Grand Marnier. People must like vodka, I figured, because there were four Absoluts and four Stolis. A couple of Bailey's and a couple of Dry Sacks, too. Two Buds, two Millers and a Heineken to wash it all down.

I opened a mini-bottle of Chivas and raised it to my lips. Then I put it down without taking a sip.

I poured it into the toilet. One by one, I followed with the others. $287 flushed down the drain. Then I walked back over to the computer.

"He's our son," I said, winking at Eliza. "This time, I'm going to be there when it counts."

CHAPTER 31

I had no idea my fingers could move that fast. The thought of losing either Schuyler or Eliza or both was all the motivation I needed.

The San Francisco Six were finally identified. The group reportedly included two former Cybronics employees. Although both had resigned in recent months, both left letters in their homes noting their admiration for Avery Kord, to supplement the pro-Kord sentiment of the suicide note the whole group had initialed. The media portrayed them all as smart, passionate, impressionable people. Whiz kids. Schuyler could have been any one of them.

But he wasn't. He didn't attend a recent industry conference in San Francisco, as it was reported all the others did.

There was no sign of my son in Portland. The police sergeant agreed to paste posters on trees, traffic light poles, the sides of trolleys. All over Fareless Square, the heart of downtown. And he'd have a few friends do the same up in the Willamette Valley, the Oregon wine country, the mountains. He sent his regards, his best wishes, his suggestion that I join a grief group to begin the mourning process—"Just in case, Mister, Sir." But he was working on it. And on nailing Hank Driver. The man left Portland after he broke Tammy Wood's nose and cut her so badly with a broken mirror that she needed eighteen stitches across her face. When she was released from the hospital she went down to the precinct and turned over some perverted child pornography that he photographed. According to the sergeant, some of the children seemed younger than age 7 and one girl, whose face was shown as it was urinated on, still wore a diaper.

I felt good about Tammy's decision to cooperate, happy to hear the Portland cops might be able to close in on Driver. But the sergeant said Tammy didn't know anything about Sky's disappearance other than recalling my visit to the apartment. Driver had brought her there that morning and told her to keep quiet and act as if he usually lived there. The apartment was a condo that Driver owned and sublet to Cybronics, which probably accounted for why it was listed as Driver's address rather than Sky's in the Portland police computers. So to me this all was interesting but useless information.

Lucille told me that ISI still had come up with nothing about Sky. He hadn't left a trail with his credit cards or gotten any speeding tickets, so Bart Casey had no idea where he might be. But Casey had forwarded more information to her about Driver's Cayman Islands bank account.

"ISI's got a contact in the Caymans, Mr. Lightman. Some Detective Inspector down there. I don't know how they do it."

"We're not supposed to know." I tried to think of ballplayers I once knew who might have come from the Cayman Islands. None came to mind.

"Mr. Casey said the weather was great down there, really good for his back, and that he had a look at the bank records in person. He wasn't allowed to copy them."

"The trip's on me, obviously. If you talk to him again, Lucille, tell him I want a receipt for every cent."

"He's already sent a bunch, Mr. Lightman. Anyway, there have been lots and lots of small deposits into the account—a thousand here, a couple thousand there."

"Driver's into child porn and other ugly stuff, Lucille. Dirty pictures and what have you. It must be where he hides the proceeds."

"I guess. But there have been a couple of biggies, too. There was a hundred thousand dollar deposit when it was opened. May 1982. A wire transfer. Then a lot of tens and twenty thousands over the years. They add up to almost half a million, but there was no single one of big size again, until last week. Fifty thousand more."

"That's it?"

"You want to know where the wires came from? I mean the two biggies?"

"Whatever you've got, Lucille."

"Mr. Casey said he can't get names. Just places. Or one place, in this case."

"Portland, Oregon?"

"How'd you ever guess, Mr. Lightman?"

I called Yale, but there was no sign of Schuyler there. Doctor Wigman expressed his concern, wanted me to send Sky up to see him as soon as I found him. There would be more posters and a photographic ad in the Alumni Weekly.

There was no answer at Scarlett Exner's house.

No rational answer at Annie Wilnot's number, either. Just the faraway, troubled voice of a woman who had lost everything.

I tried everyone I knew, everyone I thought Sky knew. His college and high school friends. A paraplegic kid Sky had stayed in touch with since first grade. A number of his math professors. I also asked for suggestions from several of the outside lawyers we used at Terrell Finch. The senior partners at Snelmer and Pickens said they'd mull it over. Since I told them to go ahead only if it was free, I knew they wouldn't mull too long. I even placed a call up to Eno Loggia, on the off-chance that Sky went up to visit the winery. Eno's answering machine advised that he was away on vacation.

I went back to St. Andrew's Church. No recent meetings in the basement, I was advised. Father MacMillan still had my business card, knew where to call if necessary.

I didn't eat for two days. Didn't drink, either, except for frequent cups of coffee. Visited Lucille at the office. She had no luck with her phone calls, but she arranged for an 800 number: 1-800-FIND-SKY. And for publicity in airports, bus terminals, train stations. I went to the psychotherapist, the local synagogue, the local church, the local mosque. A psychic with a crystal ball refunded my fee after an hour because she said the ball was out of order. I started wearing a gold Star of David with a cross down the center. Carried a rabbit's foot.

I lost four pounds and gained black circles under my eyes like the pine tar some ballplayers use to reduce glare.

If I kept it up, I figured I'd soon be joining Eliza and Katie and the San Francisco Six and Justin Webb on some big ethereal line waiting for hors d'oeuvres. My heartbeat felt increasingly arrhythmic and I developed an annoying ringing in my ears.

I called hospitals but avoided morgues. Called every Cybronics office I could find listed in a 20-million number CD-ROM phone directory. Funny thing. A few months earlier, I wouldn't have known how to insert it into my E: drive. I wouldn't have even known which drive was my E: drive.

After three days, four days, a big blur of days, I crashed. My body gave out.

It needed sleep.

It needed nourishment.

Most of all, it needed some reason for hope.

CHAPTER 32

I dreamed I was awake.

I dreamed we were in the middle of a snowstorm, the deepest and ugliest Nor'easter in decades. Cars were buried in white piles, the doors of houses were forced shut by windy drifts, and many homeless were dying a cold white death.

Schuyler was working at a Cybronics plant in New Haven, Connecticut. He had recently been clinically depressed, according to doctors Avery Kord had recommended. The doctors couldn't quite determine why, the Prozac was proving to be just a short-term fix, and his bouts of anxiety were relentless.

"Dad," Sky said on the phone, slurring his words, "I feel like my mind's outside, watching my body in a 3-D animation sequence. Like virtual reality. It seems inevitable that I'm going to pick up a blade and cut something, wrists or ankles or something...I just can't get myself back to normal."

"Go to the hospital right now," I begged my son. "And don't tell Avery Kord which one. Go down to Hartford General."

"I'll try, Dad, if I can get up and move," he promised. "I'll have to pretend I've got a remote control for my legs or something."

"I'm coming up right away," Eliza mouthed into the extension phone. "I love you, Sky."

"I know, Mom. This just isn't about that."

After we hung up the phone, she ran to the closet and put on her coat.

"There are two feet of snow out there, Lize," I said. "There's no way to get up to New Haven. Wait 'til it's cleared."

"That could take three days or a week," she said. "He's our son."

"He's going to Hartford General."

"Cliff, I'd never forgive myself if—"

I grabbed her as she took her keys out of her coat pocket. I yelled so loud I think I damaged my vocal cords.

"Be reasonable, Eliza! There is a fucking blizzard out there!"

She just stared at me with narrowing eyes.

"Please!"

She stood there. I let go, and I let her open the door that led from inside the house to the garage. She got into the Ford Explorer and started the ignition. I walked next to the driver side door and motioned for her to roll down the window. Instead, she opened the main garage door with the remote control.

A razorsharp cold engulfed the garage as the windy white-streamed air swept in. Before I could stop her, before the clouds of my hurried breath could dissipate, the Explorer was on its way. It was elevated and had four-wheel drive, a heavy muscular vehicle, and Eliza must have felt in control. I know she wouldn't have gone if she believed otherwise.

I was frozen in more ways than one. I had no shoes on and my toes felt as if they were buried in ice; my coatless body shivered in the chill of the air.

I closed the garage door and walked back inside the house. I thought briefly. I decided first to ensure that Schuyler made it over to Hartford General. Then I'd go up after my wife.

I called Sky's number. No answer. I tried again. No answer.

I called Hartford information to get a number and tell them to get ready, but I reached a recording stating that due to the inclement weather, the administrative staff had been relieved for the day. I had barely hung up the phone when it rang.

It was Scarlett. She was talking on a cell phone from Schuyler's BMW. He was driving to Hartford General. He'd be okay until the next day. Dr. Wigman from Yale was going to meet them there.

I put on heavy woolen socks, my boots, a sweater and a down parka. I quickly tossed some extra clothes and supplies into a duffel bag, along with some chocolate kisses and a can of Coke. I turned off all the house-lights and went back to the garage. Driving the Camry in this weather would be a lot tougher than the Explorer, but I had no choice.

The Beatles sang A Day In The Life on the radio as I drove. I gripped the steering wheel so hard my cold sweaty palms froze to it and I lost a small amount of skin when I pulled them off.

When I was finally able to push the speedometer to 30 mph on I-95, I didn't go far before I started seeing a red light, turning, again and again illuminating the snow. There were no warning flares on the road, no safety triangles. Just the round red light atop a police car turning, repetitively, bathing the white snow in an eerie red glow with each revolution. Two cars in front of me had stopped, and as I inched closer to the scene, a sick phlegmatic feeling crawled into the pit of my stomach.

In the distance I could hear sirens: ambulance sirens, firetruck sirens, police sirens. I had never learned to distinguish. They got fainter and I knew they were moving away, to a hospital or, I prayed, toward the consciousness of my waking day and out of this horrible nightmare.

Frustrated, I packed a tight wet snowball together and fired a fastball at a traffic light a hundred yards away. I hit the joint that held the light fixture, the precise spot I had aimed for. The impact broke the joint so that the light swayed in the whipping gusts, attached only by its exposed wires.

I got back into my car and started to drive, getting up to ninety miles per hour but never gaining ground on the ambulance, unable to see anything but its red light glowing through the windy haze. When I arrived at the hospital she was in a coma, electrode wires connecting her shaved scalp to a brain wave monitor, a respirator tube inserted into her windpipe through a hole that appeared to have been cut by something no more precise than a hacksaw.

"Eliza," I said as I walked in.

No response.

"Shutterbug," I whispered.

She blinked.

A Radio Shack cassette player sat on the table next to her. I pushed the PLAY button and my wife's voice emerged.

"Schuyler's in the room next door, Cliff," the tape of Eliza announced. "He's dying. Tried to kill himself. Overdosed. His heart is giving out. He needs a transplant."

"What can I do, Lize?"

Charlene walked in, turned off the cassette player and felt Eliza's pulse. Then the nurse looked over at me.

"Both The Missus and your son need a heart transplant, Uncle Clay. And Katie's heart still be good and strong. She would want it used to save a life. And it be their type."

"Whose type?"

"Mrs. Clay's type, sir. And your boy's type, too, of course. He be her son."

"Then which one of them will get it?"

"That be up to you, Uncle Clay," Charlene said. "Neither your wife nor your boy be well enough to decide. That be up to you."

"Why? Why me?"

•

My sheets were drenched in a cold sweat I could feel through both my pajamas and my dream state. I was aware that I was asleep, that this was a nightmare that would end soon. But I couldn't wake myself up. I was powerless, trapped.

•

"Why me?" I again asked Charlene.

"Because you be a good man," she said.

I walked to the doorway to get some air. An old man limping behind an aluminum walker looked at me. He was stooped, his hair long and gray. He had a gray mustache and a lot of wrinkles. But he was dressed in a tie-dyed shirt, bell bottom Landlubber jeans, moccasins. Puka shells around his neck.

"At least I've lived my life," the frail old Eno Loggia said.

"Mister Clay be a good man," I heard Charlene tell Eliza inside the room.

•

I jumped out of bed, ran to the bathroom and doused my face in icy cold water. Despite it, the man who stared back at me from the vanity mirror looked tired and sick and ashen.

CHAPTER 33

I had barely taken off my coat when I unpacked the computer and set it up in the den. I no longer needed the color-coding on the wires and terminals. I still wasn't a whiz, but I had become technologically almost self-sufficient.

There was no CybroMail. No standard E-mail.

Not much regular paper mail, either, just some ads and a packet that advised me that I was in the only group from which the next Publishers Clearing House millionaire would be chosen. Also a cylindrical FedEx package that turned out to contain a bottle of Five Fingers Chardonnay, courtesy of Eno Loggia. Addressed to me as Clay Blacker, PI. Even in my tense mood, it brought a smile to my face.

The only message on the answering machine was from Scarlett. She saw a "Missing" poster of Sky on a telephone pole. She took it down and planned to hang it in her new home. Avery Kord was giving her some money so she could move to Paris soon. She didn't want to go, but she needed to. For her baby. She would pray for Schuyler and stay in touch. She would call when she got to France and explain everything.

It took awhile to get the Mom.ava program up and running. It responded less crisply than usual, and the hourglass indicating that the computer was busy seemed to last forever. I wondered if something was damaged in the trip back from Tampa. It was after midnight, but I couldn't sleep, so I tinkered until Eliza finally showed up.

She was wearing a white sweatshirt and sky blue running shorts, the shiny satiny kind. I had forgotten how great she looked in them, her legs muscular like a young figure skater's. I liked that outfit on her better than a silk teddy, a Victoria's Secret body suit, a birthday suit.

"What are you staring at?" she asked, turning, looking back over her shoulder coyly, a model on a Milan runway.

"Going for a midnight run?" I asked.

"In a manner of speaking."

"I'd like to watch. You can start now."

"No, I can't." She faced me, her voice serious, and I noticed dark circles under her eyes. "I've gone through as much virus software as possible. I'm now the carrier of a rather complicated killer cocktail."

"How will it work, Lize?"

"You're going to have to send me to every Cybronics location. Every one. It won't be me you're actually sending, but a clone of the codes I'm carrying. Digital diseases. You'll have to hit every single computer hooked into their system. The Cybronics employees and vendors who have home computers, who use the software."

"What about all the people who bought a computer with Cybronics hardware or software? That's almost every person in the United States, Eliza. And many around the world."

"I don't think we have to go that far, Cliff. Remember, it's Sky we're trying to find. He's Kord's employee. He's working on a program for Kord and Cybronics. He's going to be somewhere on the employee-based system. It's almost a sure thing."

"Kord doesn't like risk, Lize, and neither do I. Not when Schuyler's involved."

"I think this is one we have to take, Cliff. Otherwise, we'd be talking hundreds of millions of computers. For now, we try 68,000 and see if it works. And Cybronics machines are linked to plenty of others. These bugs will spread like wildfire even if we don't force them to."

"How do we know which machines are in the Cybronics network?"

"Avery Kord's an egomaniac, Cliff. He tags everything with an identifier, a code, so he can track every employee, every piece of property relating to his company. He's got a different tag for customers who buy or own or download or copy something Cybronics has created. I know the codes. I have the complete lists. And I think we shoot for the 68,000 employee-related items first."

"Okay," I said. I was far from convinced, but I knew there was no stopping her. I also knew there was no alternative.

"So you'll send out packages, Cliff. Each one contains the most up-to-the-minute, most destructive viruses from the Creation lab at Cybronics. And my explicit coded instructions to explode when opened. You'll send one package to each and every one of the sixty-eight thousand addresses. And as soon as the recipients click the mouse or hit a key to open the package—"

"Kaboom?"

"Precisely."

"But why would everyone necessarily do that, Lize?"

"Because their screens will have some kind of picture on them. Something enticing, something they'll want to open. Like a Pandora's box. I'll come up with something. But whatever they choose to do, they'll be locked in by clicking. For MORE INFORMATION, they'll click. To say NO THANKS, they'll click. MAYBE LATER—click. Or turn their machines off and click when they log back on. Or try to change screens. The beauty of this virus delivery system is that no matter what they choose, the viruses will get set off. And every Cybronics program and hard drive will become about as useful as a lump of Jell-O in a plastic box."

"What about Cybronics' main systems, Lize? Aren't they protected?"

"The mainframes? I can get into those, too. I've already decoded the firewalls and inoculation programs. And I've been studying multi-platform communications. Anything I can do in a PC, I can do in a mainframe or a laptop or a handheld if it's got a datalink."

"But Kord's got the best anti-virus software on the planet, Lize."

"Maybe. But his viruses are even more powerful. They're way out in front of the things that try to kill the little buggers. They have unique signatures that can't be recognized."

"How do you know that?"

I noticed a smirk on her face.

"Schuyler created most of the viruses," she said.

I couldn't help but laugh. I had to believe that if Sky worked on them, they were more effective than anything else.

"Suppose we successfully destroy every single program connected to Cybronics, Eliza," I said. "We crash all the hard drives, everything."

"Music to my ears," she shot back. But she anticipated my next concern. "The last thing you'll be required to do is push the button that obliterates all traces of me."

"Is that really necessary?" I could feel my lip start to twitch, the blood drain out of my face.

"It won't work otherwise, Cliff. Believe me, I wish there were some other way. But at that point, I'll be disintegrating along with Cybronics' systems anyway. You won't recognize what's left of me. And there's also another reason. The clock is ticking. You remember how Avery Kord knew when I broke into the Lightman files?"

"He knew someone did. Not necessarily that it was you."

"Right. Well, he got wise. This time, the Cybronics security guys put a tracer on me."

"So they can find you?"

She nodded. "First me, then you, Cliff. To hack into a computer file, you basically have to shake hands with the receiving system. There's no other way. Then you scan its data. Only this time, when I hacked into the virus creation databases, the Cybronics security systems put an indelible stamp on my hand. It sends out signals. When they find the source of the signals, they find me. And they've got a team right now working on it. Since my home location is this computer, which is in this house—"

My voice felt constricted by a tightening throat, but I managed to get my words out.

"How do we know we'll get Sky back," I asked, "even if we screw up the entire system?"

"We don't, Cliff." Eliza didn't hesitate. "But it'll give us our best shot. First, we'll be destroying the subliminal suggestion program. So he won't receive any signals directing him to try suicide. The suggestion will disappear. So that eliminates possible Plan A. As for Plan B, once their systems start falling apart, you'll have some time. I'm not sure how you'll find him. But at that point, it'll be up to you." She looked down. Her smile was gone.

"I love you, Shutterbug," I said, touching the screen with my fingertips. Then I leaned forward and lightly kissed the image of her cheek.

"Let's go," she said as I pulled back. "The faster you pull off a Band-Aid, the less it hurts."

CHAPTER 34

Eliza winked and the screen turned page white. A few seconds ticked by. Then she reappeared in a small window in the upper right corner, but she was still and silent as the e-mail addresses began to scroll by:

AAaron@CYB.com
AAbbe@CYB.gov.com
AAbbott@CYB.com.htp
AAbdul@CYB.edu

My screen quickly filled, and kept scrolling down about ten lines per second as more and more CybroMail addresses raced across its bottom line.

ABrudne@CYB.edu
WBryan@CYB.com
RBurns@CYB.edu
DBurpee@CYB.edu
RBurr@CYB.gov.com

A horizontal bar graph on the lower left estimated that the download of information would take two more hours.

I left the machine on and took a breather outside. The brisk air was a relief after Tampa's. It was almost pitch black on the street, but far from deserted. A couple strolled hand-in-hand while an elderly lady walked her basset hound. I waited in line to buy the Saturday night edition of the Sunday *Times*. It was thick and heavy. I checked to be sure all the sections were there.

I noticed Avery Kord's face on the front page. He had testified on Friday before a Congressional committee. Congress was considering whether to break up Cybronics into smaller pieces or to bar it from certain aspects of the software and Internet businesses because it was already a huge, unfettered, abusive monopoly. Imposing restrictions would give some of the politicians' constituents, Kord's competitors, a chance to make a few bucks. It's the American way. A final committee vote was scheduled to take place in a few weeks, giving Kord's lawyers enough time to submit briefs if they wanted to. There was some talk of delay for a few months out of respect for the San Francisco Six, but most legislators thought that step unnecessary. The group was identified as on the fringe, too far out of the mainstream for their deaths to warrant a postponement of the vote.

Despite the recent tragedy and the high stakes for him, Kord smiled widely in the photo, a hint of buck teeth and his well-known oversized glasses; you would have guessed he had freckles even though I didn't notice any. Middle America had to love the guy. He was your annoying little brother having the last laugh, making good, the kind of kid who probably ate the shepherd's pie in the school cafeteria and liked it. How could such an innocent face mask the soul of a criminal so evil that he would somehow arrange to kill his own partner and at least two of his most promising proteges? Yet just to be sure you love him, just in case you still had a reasonable doubt, he was appearing on *60 Minutes* tonight to show you his house, his minivan, his dog. His toys. And he'd give you an on-line present. This would be Avery Kord Lite. And live. Not prerecorded. He wanted the public to know this was the real, flesh-and-blood, unrehearsed thing.

On impulse, anxiety, I flipped to the obituaries as I walked down the street. I felt a wave of relief when I saw no Lightmans. Still, I chewed my lower lip as I marched home, Avery Kord safely under my arm. I felt some kind of perverse satisfaction by knocking his face with my elbow as I took each step.

I also wondered about the wire transfers into Hank Driver's Cayman Islands account. The string of thousands, maybe even the tens and twenties, must have been for porn. But there were the biggies. They were obviously payments. The first one came soon after Justin Webb's murder. So Kord might well have paid for his partner's murder, and Driver surely seemed to have the disposition to pull it off. This time around, I figured

Driver got smarter and wanted half up front. I shuddered to think what the recent fifty thousand might be a down payment for, but I thanked God there wasn't any record of another fifty.

Not yet.

I got home as the program reached the addresses at the tail of the alphabet:

Hwieland@CYB.com
KWilnot@CYB.com
PWright@CYB.com
FXavier@CYB.org.edu
EYale@CYB.com
Tyounger@CYB.edu

Then, finally:

VZwingli@CYB.edu
VZworykin@CYB.org.edu

Then it flashed, in bold blue letters:

THIS FILE HAS BEEN SUCCESSFULLY DOWNLOADED!

Eliza had been frozen for more than two hours. Now she emerged from her cryogenic state, but remained on the screen only in a little corner window.

"Okay, Cliff," she said, some color filling her white cheeks. "Now you scroll back up to page one. That's 3,011 pages. You highlight the first address and hit SEND."

Scrolling back up took a couple of minutes. This was a big job even for Sky's state-of-the-art Cybronics machine.

"Kord's puss is in the paper," I said while repeatedly hitting the up arrow key. "He just testified because Congress is thinking about putting some restrictions on his business. They're voting in a couple of weeks."

Her lips curled before she spoke. "A ball and chain on his ankles for ten to twenty might help."

"His *60 Minutes* appearance is tonight, Lize. A live broadcast. He's going to send a present to everybody in the universe with a modem. Just like his father told me. He announced it in the *Times*."

Eliza frowned. "Did you hear what you just said?"

I felt my brow furrow.

"Cliff, what kind of gift do you think he's going to transmit to everyone?"

My finger froze at NMacchia@CYB.com.

"Subliminal suggestion? Lize, you don't suppose—"

"It's a live show, so he has to do it in a way that isn't obvious. He doesn't control the show, the production. But he does control the gizmos he's planning to show off and the surprise gift he's going to send everyone over the Internet."

"You really think he plans to send out subliminal suggestions?"

"Why not? It's perfect. He sends millions of people something he knows they'll open because they've seen the show. And they're thrilled, whatever it is. Probably copies of some of the paintings he owns, the Van Goghs and Picassos and Rembrandts. Screen savers. And as you stare at them, you don't even realize that he's twisting your brain to make you go out and buy fifty more of his company's products."

Her face and her lips turned redder. "If you're in Congress, he's sending you subliminal instructions to vote against harming his business. You use your computer over the next few weeks, it leaves an indelible mark on your point of view. An invisible mark. Everyone thinks it's all just because they liked him as he appeared on the boob tube."

I knew she was right. The timing of the television appearance and the novel idea of sending everyone an E-mail gift just a few weeks before the Congressional vote was too coincidental.

"Assuming the worst, Cliff, then Sky's program's got to be in place and ready to go by tonight. And I'm pretty sure Kord would want to keep Sky around in case of a foul-up. So Schuyler's either finished testing it or is racing to complete it even as we speak."

I nodded. "Sky's probably holed up with a computer somewhere right now." I didn't want to consider the possibility that the testing had already been done. I clung to the notion that there was still time.

Eliza started to vocalize my thoughts. "Once he's completed the work, Cliff—"

"I know, Lize. We need to move fast."

I scrolled all the way back up to AAaron@CYB.com. I highlighted the address, moved the cursor to the SEND button and clicked the mouse.

The screen bleeped for a second before YOUR MESSAGE HAS BEEN SENT appeared.

I repeated the process for AAbbe@CYB.gov.com, then for AAbbott@CYB.com.htp. The process was cumbersome, and it was already 2:30 in the morning. I didn't need Sky's math ability to calculate that at that pace, I'd be unable to finish by the time *60 Minutes* came on. I knew there had to be a more efficient way, but I didn't know how. Eliza was again in suspended animation in the corner window. Her image seemed coarser, out of focus. I figured she was tired.

Or something like that.

I tried highlighting five addresses at a time before clicking on SEND. The machine froze for about a second, barely longer than for just a single address, and then advised that the messages had been sent. I tried ten. This time it froze too long, so long I thought the whole system would crash and I'd lose all of it. I decided it was safer to stay with five addresses on each shot. This was no time for careless chances. I still had to get from the B's through the Z's.

CHAPTER 35

The sun rose outside my den window, casting the gray keyboard in a yellow glow made softer by the sheer curtains Eliza had picked out many years earlier. I got up for a cold one-minute shower, brushed my teeth, made some coffee. I was tired, nervous, anxious; the taste in my mouth reminded me of burning tires. Five minutes attending to some human needs would keep me as alert and efficient as possible.

When I sat down and looked at the monitor, Eliza was gone. The little window she had been in had also disappeared. There was nothing in its place but a continuation of the screen's white background.

"Lize," I called out.

Nothing.

"Eliza!" I raised my voice. Nothing.

"Shutterbug!" The volume might have woken the neighbors, but I had my priorities. Their kids were all safely tucked in.

Still nothing.

I was tempted to turn off the machine or exit and start up again. But the names were still up on the screen, I had around 46,000 more messages to mail, and I was scared that if I shut down, I'd lose all that data.

And I'd lose my son.

I hoped it was a temporary glitch, but I had a feeling that Kord's experts had gotten to Eliza. Found out she broke into the virus creation lab.

I wasn't sure if they could trace her back to my house, my phone numbers, but I figured they could. And I didn't know whether they had any idea what she was doing with the viruses she stole.

I didn't know much of anything, to tell you the truth.

I wondered whether there was an electronic equivalent of water torture, of bamboo shoots under the fingernails, of ways to interrogate her under hot lights, to make her talk.

Or whether they'd do those things to me, if they managed to track me down. It wouldn't take much to torture me. My head was pounding and I had enough acid in my stomach to refill a car battery.

But Eliza and I had a plan, and I was intent on keeping up my end of it.

I highlighted the next five e-mail addresses and clicked SEND. The screen froze for a second, then declared in bold: YOUR MESSAGES HAVE BEEN SENT.

I was back in business.

My fingers mechanically highlighted names, double-clicked the mouse on SEND, highlighted the next group of names.

My mind wandered back to the days when we taught Schuyler the Alphabet Song. We once had a heated debate over whether the song should end with "tell me what you think of me," which is how I learned it, or "next time won't you sing with me," which I viewed as a corruption but Eliza thought was more nurturing.

One Fish, Two Fish, The Cat In The Hat, Are You My Mother?, Horton Hears A Who, Hop On Pop. Titles and shiny red and blue and yellow covers raced through my mind, along with exaggerated illustrations of odd animals: Sneetches and Zax and Foxes in Boxes.

I had gotten through the P's by four o'clock in the afternoon. The process was slower than I had expected. Still no sign of Eliza. I wondered where Eno had gone on vacation. Whether Bart Casey had returned from the Caymans.

The *60 Minutes* program was scheduled to begin at seven. I had completed sixteen letters of the alphabet in fourteen hours. Ten letters left; only three more hours. I would have to quicken the pace. And hope nothing went wrong. Of course, I still had the R's and S's and T's. I remembered from my Scrabble-playing days that more words began with those than any other letters. But these were names, not words, so I didn't know if the same principles applied.

I tried to work faster, tried groups of six instead of five. Held down the mouse button on a single long click rather than double-clicking. I don't know whether it made a difference. But before I got through with the S's, Eliza reappeared.

She was paler, duller, marred by stray dots that would have been called snow in the days of rabbit-ears and *Leave It To Beaver*.

She was also upset, breathing heavily.

"There's no time to finish, Cliff," she said, her voice fainter. You have to destroy me. Now."

I was off-guard; it was premature. Her absence had permitted me to ignore this part of the plan, make believe it wouldn't be necessary.

"Where were you?"

"Split up into ten different hiding places. To make myself harder to locate. But the codes that enable me to exist as the image you see were all tagged when I cloned the viruses. They're all traceable. And the tracking software is decoding me. I can sense it. They'll figure it out. You've got to do it before it's too late, Cliff. For you and for Sky."

"But I haven't completed the alphabet! What if his CybroMail address starts between T and Z?"

"No time."

"Okay. What do I do?"

"It's not hard. You exit CybroMail. You click on the icon that looks like a little file cabinet. It lists all the files. You click on "Mom.ava." Another little menu pops up. And you click on Uninstall. It asks if you're sure you want to uninstall the program. You click on Yes. Then the process takes a minute or two. It may ask you again if you're sure. You answer in the affirmative."

I stared at her.

"I don't want to lose you a second time, Eliza."

"It's our only chance," she said. "And Sky's."

Then she smiled.

"What on earth could be so funny?" I asked, wiping a palmful of sweat beads off my forehead.

"If we were going to be in Casablanca," she said, "I always thought I'd play Ilsa. Not Rick. But I have an irresistible urge to tell you that if you don't uninstall me soon, you'll regret it—maybe not today, maybe not tomorrow, but soon and for the rest of your life."

I felt a widening grin I couldn't stop. Through all of it, she was still the Eliza Briggs I had married.

"We'll always have Paris," I said. I gripped the mouse hard. My clammy palm trembled as it maneuvered the cursor to exit the program. Eliza winked and mouthed a kiss as I quietly whispered, "I love you, Shutterbug."

Then the screen went blank just before I puked all over the keyboard, hit my head on the corner of the desk and passed out.

CHAPTER 36

"Pretty complicated machine you have there," said a very tall man with a long slender neck, one of four men, two very tall and two very short. Each of them had a big silver crescent decorating the back of his white nylon jacket like a team emblem. As my vision crept back into focus I realized there were only two intruders.

"Expensive looking," said the one who was shorter by two feet but had a voice like an electric bass compared to the big guy's tin whistle. The short guy was also considerably rounder and had spiked hair that looked as if he had sucked it dry with a vacuum cleaner hose.

"You pay extra for the vomit on the keyboard?" said the one I started to think of as Giraffe.

"Hey, fella," said Hedgehog—you know which one he was—pointing to my cheek. "Looks like you had a pretty bad fall there."

"And a worse winter," I quipped, my knees cracking as I pulled myself up in an effort to sit lotus-style on my rug. My head felt as if a 3-year old was pounding colorful wooden shapes through it with a wooden hammer.

"Why don't you wash up," said Giraffe, or the bulging Adam's apple which I wasn't sure he controlled, or both. "Then we've got a few matters to discuss."

The icy bathroom water brought some circulation back to my face, cleared off the blood that had dried near my mouth. My cheek was swollen from its ill-planned rendezvous with the edge of my desk.

It was already five-thirty.

When I walked back into the den, I noticed that the keyboard was clean. Hedgehog saw me staring at it.

"Washed it," he said. "These expensive babies can withstand a little water."

"What do you guys want?" I asked. "Last time I looked, this was my house."

"Maybe," said Giraffe. "But it's got something of ours in it."

"Yeah," said Hedgehog. "Viruses. Car bombs and Trojan Horses and Pandora's Boxes. To name a few. Top-notch stuff."

"Viruses?" I tried to look incredulous. "Come closer, I'll sneeze on you."

"Don't play dumb, Mister Lightman. We know you're a hacker. Anybody who could break through our firewall—"

"With a system this sophisticated—"

"And with our viruses—"

"Okay," I said, nodding. I held up my hands, "I surrender" style. "How'd you find me?"

"We work in the Virus Control lab," said Giraffe. "Cybronics has two sister labs, Creation and Control."

"Right," said Hedgehog. "Our job is squelch, squash, destroy."

"But how do you know I have them?"

"Creation advised us they'd been copied," said Giraffe. "Well, Creation's not stupid. The company's state-of-the-art bugs didn't just decide to swim over here through the phone lines and take up residence."

"They're not sperm cells and this house isn't an egg," Hedgehog added.

"So Creation put a tracer on them?" I asked, trying to speak the language.

Giraffe nodded, laughed a wimpy nasal laugh for a guy whose vocal cords must have been as long as a yo-yo string.

"Even if I stole them, you guys are trespassing." I tried to sound stern, mad, as if I could do something to stop them. I don't think staring at them helped, but it was the only defense I could muster for a few moments. "So what do you want?"

"We're not criminals," said Hedgehog. "We just want what's rightfully ours."

"The computer," specified Giraffe.

I shook my head to clear it.

"The computer is mine," I said firmly. "It's the viruses that are yours."

"You might have a point there, Mister Lightman," said Hedgehog. "Tell me, how did you get a multi-million dollar computer certified for Cybronics employee-only use?" He beamed, obviously figuring he had me. So I threw the question back at him like a hot potato.

"Don't you know about me?"

Hedgehog looked up at Giraffe. Giraffe looked down at Hedgehog. They made diagonal eye contact.

"We checked employee records," said Hedgehog.

"No Cybronics employees named Lightman," said Giraffe.

"That's because I do top secret work for Avery Kord," I said, trying not to hesitate. Kord's deletion of Schuyler's personnel files had become a lucky break. "Avery doesn't want me listed on any official documents. I'm what you might call an independent contractor."

"And we're supposed to believe that?" G and H asked simultaneously, their voices an odd duet.

"Nobody works directly with Mister Kord," Hedgehog said definitively. "We barely know the guy really exists."

Giraffe nodded.

I kept the tables turned.

"I have the computer," I pointed out.

"Big deal," they both shrugged in unison.

"It wasn't reported as stolen."

They nodded a bit.

"I got over the firewall"—I borrowed their terminology, not quite sure of what it meant—"and I knew exactly how to clone your viruses. From a top secret, digitally securitized facility." I hoped I sounded like I knew what I was talking about. I also realized these guys fit Eno's description of his visitors, Ben and Jerry. "And I know all about the winery."

The nods grew more pronounced, accompanied by furrowed brows.

"None of that proves squat," Hedgehog said, sounding uncertain.

"I'm going to let you guys in on a little secret," I replied. "You can check with the company if you want. We have a Code One lab down in Tampa."

"Code One?" they both asked. Four eyes widened like saucers. Maybe I had gone a little overboard. But my year of professional (okay, minor league) pitching taught me how to act unruffled even when you don't have your best stuff. Try to fool the batters with your calm approach, get them to swing at pitches outside the strike zone. Problem now was, I didn't have any relievers warming up in the bullpen.

"Secret. Unpublished. Unnamed and unaddressed," I said, trying to keep my voice steady. "It's at the Tampa Rey cigar factory. We do work for NASA. Spy satellite software. Star Wars. Foreign intelligence. I've been there. My work's related to that. But I can't tell you exactly what I do."

"Step out for a minute," Hedgehog said, motioning me toward the door.

I obliged and shut the door behind me. I couldn't hear exactly what they were saying, but I had the sense Hedgehog knew something about Tampa and maybe I had struck a chord.

They reopened the door.

"If you've been to our Tampa facility," said Hedgehog as I walked back in, "you have a special key."

I stared at him.

He stared back, eyes narrowed to their normal shape, figuring he called my bluff.

I zipped over to my bedroom and took Katie's key ring from the top of my dresser. I also grabbed my suitcase. I carried both back to the den.

"Here's my luggage," I said, plopping the old Gladstone in front of Hedgehog. "You'll note that the most recent airline tag says Tampa-St. Pete."

"Could've gone to Busch Gardens," he said, as if he still had me.

He didn't.

"Here's the key," I said, tossing him the ring. "If you've been there, you know which one it is." He grabbed it from the air, glanced at the plastic card key, stared at me in silence.

"Well?" I finally asked.

He rubbed the card key with his thumb. Then he smiled. "At Cybronics—"

"We make life worth living." I completed his sentence.

"He's okay," Hedgehog said to Giraffe.

"But he cloned the viruses," came the high-pitched reply. "We still have a job to do."

"He's right," agreed Hedgehog. "A job." He opened his white shirt-jacket and removed a Philips screwdriver.

"Look, let me make a suggestion." I grabbed his wrist hard and the screwdriver dropped to the floor. "Avery's gonna be on t.v. soon. I'm sure we'll all want to watch him. Why don't I just e-mail all the virus clones to your office? It won't take more than a minute."

"But you'll still have copies. They're proprietary. You're not allowed. If Mister Kord wants you to have them, he'll make sure you get them some other way."

I nodded. "What if I tell you that my whole purpose was to see if I could access them? To see how long it would take you guys to track me down, so I can report back to Avery on the integrity of our virus creation, maintenance and security programs?"

They looked at each other again.

"How'd we do?"

"You caught me in less than twenty-four hours," I said. "I think the country is in great hands."

"The country?" asked Hedgehog.

"Oops," I said with a smile. "I meant the company. Although there's still room for improvement."

"You'll report to Mr. Kord that Virus Control was right on your tail?"

"Absolutely."

"Okay," said Hedgehog. "You e-mail us the viruses. We'll check with our office to be sure the package is received in the in-box. But I'm afraid I have to add another step."

"What's that?"

"You'll have to destroy your copies."

"And the program you stole them with," added Giraffe. "Our systems show a complex stealth program of some kind. Something foreign and dangerous."

"I've got them all stored in one place. The stealth program stores them. You sure I have to destroy that one, once the viruses are gone?" I asked.

"Good cops wouldn't leave a car thief with his crowbar," he replied.

"You wouldn't want to cost us our jobs," added Hedgehog. "We've got to follow S.O.P."

"I hear you," I replied. "Hey, would you guys like a beer?"

"Nah," said Giraffe. "We're on the job."

"Just testing," I said. "I'll be sure you get another credit in your personnel files."

I walked up to the computer. The monitor was blank. Now I was playing their ballgame. I hoped I could fake it. I double-clicked the mouse. CybroMail appeared. The list of addresses scrolled right to the point at which I had left off.

"You're into your e-mail directory already?" asked Hedgehog.

"This guy's good," commented Giraffe. 'Look, his directory contains only Cybronics addresses."

"What's your address?" I asked.

MIND GAMES

"VIRUSBUSTERS," said Giraffe.

"Never would have guessed," I laughed, wondering if he meant VIRUSBUSTERS@CYB.com. I scrolled down. That address actually appeared. I highlighted the name and hit SEND. In about a second, the screen read: YOUR MESSAGE HAS BEEN SENT. Just like the thousands of others I had been sending.

"Good show," said Hedgehog. "Now I have to call to get confirmation."

He started toward my phone, then stopped and unclipped his own cellphone from his belt instead. He made his call and was advised that a new CybroMail message had been received. Unlike a regular message, he was told, the new one appeared as an icon resembling a blue Tiffany's box with a white ribbon tied around it. Eliza's handiwork.

"I like your style," Hedgehog said as he clicked off the phone. "Now let's get rid of your virus file and the theft program."

I sat in my chair in front of the monitor. I tried to recall exactly what Eliza told me to do to uninstall her. I exited CybroMail and saw a little icon that resembled a file cabinet. I clicked and it listed a large number of files. I scrolled down to Mom.ava and highlighted it.

I was about to double-click the mouse when I heard Hedgehog's husky voice from above and behind me.

"This thing is called MOM?" he asked.

I thought about it for a few seconds. I couldn't remember what Schuyler said MOM stood for.

"Mind Over Matter," I said, trying to sound nonchalant.

"You hackers sure are creative," said Giraffe.

"I'm not exactly a hacker," I said. "I'm in the same business as you."

"Security?" Giraffe asked.

I nodded.

"Then you will understand why we have to kill you," said Giraffe, pulling a black revolver out of an inner pocket of his nylon Cybronics jacket and jamming it into my temple. He pressed so hard I thought he'd leave a hole even without pulling the trigger. I knew his immediate intent was to force me out of my desk chair. Needless to say, I quickly obliged.

"We just can't have people hacking around, breaking in, cracking Cybronics codes," Giraffe said.

"But thanks for highlighting the virus theft program," said Hedgehog, assuming my seat in front of the monitor. "Now that we know which one it is, we'll take it apart and learn exactly how you did it."

CHAPTER 37

"I clicked but it won't start up," said Hedgehog. "Something's wrong. The usual code sequences won't bypass the password requirement. And I can't find any back doors."

"Maybe we should try a core dump," offered Giraffe. He had pulled the muzzle off of my temple and moved behind me, but I could see in the hall mirror that he kept the gun pointing at my head at a downward angle like Oswald's bullet through Kennedy. Funny what you remember from college.

"That could fuck it up for good," Hedgehog answered. "We might never be able to reconfigure the data."

"You need the password," I said, uncertain of what they were talking about but able to breathe a little deeper anyway.

"Nah," said Hedgehog. "We'll just take the whole computer to the lab and study the program at our convenience."

"Yeah," said Giraffe. "Posthumously."

He laughed and walked around in front of me, keeping the revolver aimed at my head. From my vantage point, the barrel looked like the Holland Tunnel.

"Say your prayers," Hedgehog said, holding his wrist up and looking at his watch. "You have exactly one minute."

It was clear Giraffe wouldn't have much reluctance to pull the trigger. I wished I was with someone I loved. I was running out of time.

"Shutterbug!" I shouted as loudly and clearly as I could.

Hedgehog turned to stare at me.

"Shutterbug!" I repeated.

"What kind of prayer is that?" Giraffe asked.

"It's not," I said. "It's the password."

Hedgehog turned to type it but Eliza's face appeared on the monitor. She was frozen like a close-up photograph.

"What the fuck is this?" he asked.

"It's Mom.ava," I answered. "The virus theft program."

"A picture of a woman?" Giraffe asked, suddenly mesmerized, staring at the screen, holding onto the gun but dropping his hand to his side. I gauged him a bit too far away for me to make a credible lunge for it. I did manage to pick up the screwdriver Hedgehog had dropped earlier. "Where the hell are all the alphanumeric codes, the CybroSymbols, the script and equations?"

"They're all there," I said, inching a bit closer to him. "I just wanted a more pleasant user interface."

"You're full of shit," said Hedgehog.

"He's actually not," said Eliza, suddenly animated, her image crystal clear, her voice matter-of-fact and very much alive. "Not to mention that this house is carefully monitored, wired and bugged. If you do not begin immediately to listen to Mr. Lightman's instructions, you will be arrested and taken into custody. Or worse."

My two visitors again made diagonal eye contact.

"Define 'worse,'" said Giraffe.

"Just hand Mister Lightman the gun," Eliza said. "Or neither of you will ever leave this house alive."

"This is a trick," said Hedgehog, his voice almost as squeaky as his big buddy's.

Giraffe shook his head from side to side. "Never saw a computer program do this," he said.

"This is not just a program," Eliza said. "You men are on video surveillance. And are being tape-recorded. Duplicates are being made at a location I will not disclose. They'd make great copy for the 7 o'clock news, no?"

Hedgehog pointed at the optical sensors on top of the monitor and nodded as if he now understood. "What if we leave now?" he asked.

"I want the big ugly guy to hand Mister Lightman the gun," Eliza repeated. "Then march your butts straight out of his house."

"It's just a cigarette lighter anyway," the big man said as he handed it to me. It felt heavy for a cigarette lighter. I pointed it squarely at his chest, which for me was eye-level. I told Hedgehog to stand next to him, then told them both to turn around. They did. I dug the gun into Giraffe's backside and the screwdriver into Hedgehog's upper back. They couldn't see which was which. I pushed them as they skulked toward the front door.

"One of you guys has a screwdriver sticking into him," I announced. "And the other one has a gun." My blood pressure was up, my face red. I trembled and shook as waves of acid spewed out of the pit of my gut, melding together the years of angst about my failure as a pitcher, my guilt about Eliza's accident and my feelings of impotence in my ability to save my son.

"I am going to pull the trigger," I said, not certain I meant it.

"I told you it's not real," Giraffe said, his voice wavering.

"Avery will be pleased," I said. "You did a fine job tracking me down. Most cybercops would have taken more than 24 hours."

"You gonna show Mister Kord the tape of this session?" asked Hedgehog.

"You want me to?"

"Wouldn't mind," he replied, some depth returning to his voice. "A guy needs to do something to distinguish himself in this company."

"Yeah," said Giraffe. "Virus Busters are a dime a dozen these days."

"Then I will," I said, jabbing both of them simultaneously. "Now open the door, little guy."

Hedgehog turned the knob and swung the door open. We stood just inside the doorway.

"I probably should test your equipment," I said, jamming the gun and the screwdriver into them from behind. The screwdriver dug so hard into Hedgehog I could see a small spot of red blood seep into his white nylon jacket. But even though I desperately wanted to pull the trigger, I pulled the gun away instead. I forcefully shoved them both out the door, kicking Giraffe in the back of the knee on his way out. He tripped over the doorsill and fell so hard he had a limp when he stood back up.

I locked up and watched my visitors scamper away through a little window next to the door. I noticed a corner of the glass was broken and I figured these guys had done it to gain entry. Not a big job to fix. And it could wait. I had a strong feeling G and H wouldn't be chancing a return trip anytime soon.

CHAPTER 38

I walked back into the den.

"Nice work, Batman," Eliza said.

"I think I'm Robin," I said.

"Either way, we're overdue. And *60 Minutes* is going to start soon."

I walked up to the screen and kissed my wife's image softly. She closed her eyes and I closed mine. In my mind she was real, warm flesh and coursing blood, and I would no sooner forget this kiss than our first one, in Washington Square Park, with a Beatles sound-alike band playing Yesterday for quarters.

That first night, we went back to my place and watched The Wizard of Oz on t.v. I still recall her remark that the smartest of the group, the scarecrow with his new brain, is the only one who says nothing at all as they kiss Dorothy goodbye and send her back to Kansas.

I imitated him and remained quiet.

So did my beautiful, incomparable, wonderful wife.

I won't bother you with the details of the precise sequence of computer commands I followed.

Let's just say I clicked a few times, and she was gone.

CHAPTER 39

The first thing that struck me was that Avery Kord was wearing a golf shirt and jeans. Not a suit, like most *60 Minutes* guests. When you have sixty or seventy billion dollars, you don't have to try to impress anyone. His glasses were still too big, too. He obviously hadn't talked to an image consultant. Or maybe he had, and imperfection was the name of the game. Without his bank and securities accounts, he could be the boy next door.

He spoke for a few minutes about computers, how they've changed the world. They certainly changed his world. The show was broadcast live, so to be safe he was obviously starting with material he felt comfortable with—the stuff I had heard him say on the airplane about how entire libraries would someday be downloadable from the Internet, how cars would drive themselves according to pre-programmed routes. How computers were being used to design better heart valves and jet engines, study everything from the universe to the atom, predict the weather and the outcome of a war. He pointed out that he was still a young guy with a lot of ideas that could ease everybody's life in the future—if Congress doesn't hamstring him by putting the kibosh on some of Cybronics' businesses.

I admired his style—he referred subtly but deftly to the Congressional hearings, deflecting direct questions about his business practices "because this show is not the right forum." He pointed out that the computer business is the most competitive business in the world, and he was sorry so many people suffered from a disease he called CybroPhobia. He also expressed deep remorse about the six people who committed suicide in San Francisco.

"Who can account for the vagaries of the human mind?" he humbly asked. "A terrible tragedy, but this business sometimes affects people who are so smart, who possess such great gifts, that they cannot cope in traditional ways."

The formalities out of the way, he started to get more personal. "This is my family," he said, hitting a remote control button that caused a wall-sized screen to pop up. I thought I noticed a small image of a Tiffany's box on the screen, which he quickly flipped off to get the picture he had planned. "My wife Regina, and my daughter Crystal." The pair waved in unison and each spoke tritely. Harry Cardinsky, not surprisingly, wasn't present; although the old man had put on a good face for me, I figured his perpetual anonymity had to hurt. He was watching the show, no doubt, but it must have been bittersweet for him.

"Before we move on and I show you some of the conveniences we all will soon enjoy," Kord took over, "some of the things we're working on here in our most advanced laboratories at Cybronics, let me also mention something nationally that even our friends don't know yet. Regina's pregnant again!"

"That's wonderful," came the reply of the blonde anchorwoman whose name I forget. I was convinced there was nothing this creep wouldn't do to escape having his business restricted by Congress. "Do you have a name picked out?"

"Well, I'd rather not tell you if it's a boy or a girl," came the crackly-voiced reply. "Then again," he chuckled, "I suppose I could say Pat or Chris without giving up much. But the truth is, we don't really know yet."

He held out the remote control and pointed it at the big screen his family still waved on. "This is my living room wall," he said, pushing another button. "Suppose I want to see Van Gogh's *Starry Night*." Sure enough, the screen was soon filled by clouds of blue and black and yellow. "Or *The Scream*, by Edward Munch." The image quickly changed to the famous little pained swirling man on a bridge. "Or the *Mona Lisa*." There was the mysterious smile we all knew. "I can even animate these reproductions, make them talk. Or sing. Leonardo would have loved this."

He clicked a button.

"You want to play *Clue*?" asked Mona Lisa, her mouth moving.

"What was that she said?" asked the anchorwoman as her eyebrows rose an inch. "I'm not sure I heard her."

He hit the button again.

"Would you prefer *Monopoly*?" Mona Lisa asked, loud and clear. "Or have we already won that one?"

Kord blushed so deeply I wondered whether my t.v. set needed adjusting. "I guess we still need to work out the kinks," he said, visibly sweating, trying to come back with a forced smile. "Believe me, that was unexpected. Maybe a hacker got into my system." He brushed the hair back from his forehead with a shaky palm. I wondered how many billions he was about to lose in the value of his Cybronics stock.

"Why don't we go out to your minivan," said the anchorwoman, obviously trying to keep her guest from falling further apart. "We've all been waiting for this."

"Okay," said Kord. "And I can't tell you how sorry I am about that little incident. Just to protect everyone out there, I guess I won't send out the little Internet gifts I promised. We'll save them until we find the source of the problem."

They took a commercial break, during which I listened from my bathroom to a Cybronics advertisement in which a happy little kid gets a computer for Christmas. I had seen it before. As he sits in front of the screen and bangs on the keyboard, his smiling face morphs into that of an older man—Albert Einstein.

I flushed just as the tag line came on. But I had no desire to hear it. Everyone in the world already knew that at Cybronics, they make life worth living.

When the show returned, Kord and the anchorwoman were seated in his minivan. Kord was in the driver's seat. They pulled out of his driveway and headed down the block.

"Say I'd like to hear Beethoven's Fifth," Kord announced. A computerized sound system promptly began to play it at a low volume.

"Vehicles will soon be able to follow verbal commands, read your E-mail to you, make phone calls through the sound system," he said. "And in the future, cars will even drive themselves according to programmed routes. We don't have the roads set up yet to accomplish that. Maybe satellites will send the signals. We're working out the details at Cybronics. But I've created a prototype for several miles around my house."

He pushed a button on the dashboard and a monitor screen popped up near the steering wheel. It showed a local map. "Let's say you want to go here," he said, pointing to a spot on the screen. "I touch the screen with my finger—" he did—"and that's where we go." A little "X" appeared on the screen where he touched it. "If I wanted to, now I could go to sleep until we arrive."

"What about traffic?" the anchorwoman asked. "Other cars?"

"There are sensors built in," Kord replied. "Infrared and radar. And a little digital guide I can talk to. A bot, which is short for digital robot. It acts almost like a human."

Kord hit a button and a colorful little man appeared on the screen. His t-shirt was tie-dyed, his tanned neck surrounded by puka shells. I knew the mustached face.

The minivan stopped at a red light. A sport utility vehicle stopped catty-corner from it.

"This bot reminds me of something out of the Sixties," said the anchorwoman, smiling.

"What do you think, Bart?" Kord asked the digital robot. "You something out of the Sixties?"

"Nah," came the reply. "I like to think of myself as a creature of the new millennium."

The light changed.

"We're supposed to go right!" screamed Kord, just as his minivan turned left, sped up, and plowed into the oncoming SUV.

"Shit!" yelled Kord, his face contorting, his eyes clamping shut. The sounds of screeching wheels, shattering glass and crunching metal filled my living room as the televised picture flipped over and around like the drum of a clothes dryer, landed upside down, then went black and was promptly converted into the network interruption signal, a series of horizontal pastel lines accompanied by a loud and annoying whine.

I hope nobody is seriously hurt, was my first thought, as I realized the accident had been caused by the viruses my wife had infected Kord's systems with.

Way to go, Eliza! was my second.

CHAPTER 40

Within minutes, the breaking news was interrupting every regularly-scheduled broadcast on all networks. Avery Kord had been in a televised accident. He was in serious condition, as was the *60 Minutes* anchorwoman. The accident was caused by faults in his computer network.

By Monday morning, the focus of the news had shifted. Kord would survive physically, but as a corporate visionary his status had plummeted from high-flier to bottom-fisher. Cybronics was hemorrhaging. Its computers all over the world were failing, making miscalculations. Word processors were unable to spell correctly, or were randomly inserting words, curses, yesses and no's. And systems linked to Cybronics were also experiencing difficulties. A space shuttle flight was delayed because its computers would do nothing but play tic-tac-toe with each other. Lawyers couldn't print out accurate contracts, television and radio stations couldn't control the content of the shows they broadcast. People trying to download the Bible from the Internet received copies of *Lolita* instead. The world's stock markets had massive problems because of faulty information flows; nevertheless, the price of Cybronics stock fell from $100 a share to less than $1 in a day, meaning that Avery Kord had become a mere millionaire overnight. It seemed likely he'd soon be virtually wiped out. In an act of sympathy, Congress voted to delay its upcoming vote on limiting his business. As a practical matter, the issue had become as moot as whether to save the dodo bird.

I walked into my kitchen to pour a glass of Five Fingers Chardonnay. I raised it to my lips, took in the bouquet. I silently toasted Eliza. Before taking a sip, though, I carefully poured it back into the bottle and recorked it. It was premature to celebrate.

My son was still missing.

CHAPTER 41

I was putting the bottle back in the fridge when it dawned on me: maybe Eno wasn't trying to be cute when he shipped it to me as Clay Blacker, PI. He knew I used that name when I was looking for my son; maybe he was trying to send me a signal of some kind. In a hurry. I couldn't imagine why else he'd have sent it by FedEx and not through the mails or UPS, which were cheaper. Under normal circumstances, there would be no rush. And he knew I was on the wagon; why not send me the alcohol-free stuff?

I called the telephone number set forth in small print on the back label of the wine bottle. A digital operator told me politely that it was out of service or had been temporarily disconnected.

The Taconic Parkway is full of twists and turns, but they all blurred by, along with a deer I missed by an inch. It was already Monday night, so I guess the state troopers were home watching the late football game.

As I approached the winery entrance, I turned off the headlights and slowed to a crawl. I parked near the gate, a few hundred yards from the main building that housed Eno's office. A bright floodlight lit the area near the front door, which was closed like the wooden shutters. The blackboard on the door now announced: CLOSED FOR VACATION. It seemed the lights inside were out; the only illumination emanated from the blue radiance of Eno's computer monitor. Although it was dark and the windows were few and high, I crawled the last hundred feet so as not to take any chances on casting long shadows or being seen.

I stood on a boulder near the corner of a window on the side of the building and peeked through a crack in the shutter.

I could make out only the outlines of four people. As my eyes adjusted to the dim light, I could see that two of them sat on the floor in the center of the room, each bound at the hands and feet by ropes.

Schuyler and Scarlett.

The other two wore white nylon jackets with a big Cybronics "C" emblem on their backs. One, a husky muscular guy with what appeared to be a pistol in his hand, stood a few feet away from them near the head of a long wooden table. A few wine bottles and wine glasses sat on a checked tablecloth, along with several jars of wine jelly and an open box of crackers. On the other side of the table, seated in one of the old wooden chairs, was the fourth person. Harry Cardinsky. He faced Scarlett and my son, and he was holding an open wine bottle. Nearer to me, Eno slumped over his desk. Bottles were broken and overturned all around him, and it was clear he had put up a struggle. But a shiny dark red substance ran in streaks down the side of his face, slickening and matting his hair. He was motionless.

My muscles taut with fear, I crawled back around to the front near the door. It was an old warped wooden door with a lot of cracks and wormholes, but not enough space for me to see anything. I pressed my ear against it. I could hear Scarlett's nervous voice wavering, interspersed with sobs and loud attempts to catch her breath.

"You said you were driving me up here to get the money!" she screamed. "I was going to move to France!"

"I told you that's all changed now," Harry said.

"So you would kill your own grandson?"

"Sad, but irrelevant." Harry spoke in a cold slow monotone, barely resembling the animated motormouth I recalled describing Cindy and Mindy on the shuttle bus. "You tried to use that baby to blackmail Avery!"

"No I didn't! It was Avery's idea to give me the money, so I could take the baby out of the country and raise him and you'd never hear a peep from him or me again! I promised him that! But I need the money to do it right, to do it well."

"We don't have a million dollars to give away right now."

The big man with the gun quickly announced, "You better have the fucking hundred thousand we talked about, or I'll rip that fucking heart back out with my bare hands." His voice was gruff and vaguely familiar, although I couldn't quite place it.

"You already got the first half," Harry replied. "You still have to earn the rest." He was plainly trying to steady his voice and remain in control.

"As for you, Miss Exner, I don't know what was between you and my son. But sooner or later, that child's going to want something. They always do. Or you will. Avery's going to have enough problems putting his public image back together without such issues. If he ever can. I can't take the chance that he will be ruined again someday."

"Be reasonable," I heard Schuyler say, his speech slurred as if he was drunk. "We'll all work something out."

"I already have worked it out," Harry said. "I'm not like my son, always relying on the high-tech stuff. Kid never learned his lesson. Life's not a game of chance. Sometimes you have to do things the old fashioned way."

"Or pay somebody else to," growled the other voice.

"Shut up," Harry yelled, agitated. "I'm too old to take much more shit from you."

There was no reply.

"Okay," Harry continued in his softer, sarcastic tone. "This'll all make great press, no? The deal is, Schuyler, you found out your girlfriend got pregnant by someone else. No question about that, just take a look at that big belly of hers! You got yourself good and drunk. Then you snapped and killed her. Her boyfriend too, that wino lying dead over there. After that, you took your own life. I'll leak a bit of your past history of depression and alcohol abuse just to be sure the papers get it right. And a lovey-dovey picture of the two of you. Maybe it's a couple years old, but so what? The recent problems at Cybronics and the fact your father has reported you missing won't hurt, either. And that little cult suicide thing some of your friends did out in San Francisco, that gave you some ideas, too. It all adds to the ring of truth, don't you think?"

"I didn't know any of those people," Schuyler slurred.

"Ah, but the world doesn't have to know that! And right now, Schuyler, your blood alcohol level's about three times the norm. Well past legally intoxicated. That's just about right for the medical examiner. If you'd like some more wine to help you deal with it, just ask Hank."

"How about it, kid?" laughed the crude voice I finally recognized as that of Hank Driver, the creep from my son's apartment in Portland. "You can never be too rich or too drunk! How about another funnel full?"

Schuyler started screaming, gurgling, and I imagined Driver was forcing more alcohol down my son's throat. Since that job required both hands, I figured Driver had probably put his gun down.

I didn't know what to do, how much time I had. I didn't think I had much. I grabbed the doorknob with one sweaty palm, grasped Giraffe's gun with the other. I wished I had tested it out.

I turned my wrist and felt the door handle give. I knew the door could be coaxed open. It creaked. Eno's horse, which I hadn't seen, neighed loudly from somewhere behind me.

"Somebody's here," Harry yelled.

I couldn't buy any more time. I thrust open the door with as much force as I could and bolted into the room. Bright light from the floodlamp streamed in. Harry lifted his hands to shield his eyes. So did Driver, but not before dropping a wine bottle near Schuyler and pulling his pistol out of his waistband. As I rushed in, Driver flailed around and sent a couple of shots in my direction. They missed, but shattered several bottles of wine on the table between us. Shards of glass and alcohol sprayed around the room. Streams of red and white wine showered the walls and decorated the tablecloth from one end to the other. A piece of glass shot into my left hand like shrapnel. I winced but tried to ignore the intense pain it sent up my forearm.

I ran to the wine tasting table and shoved it with all my might into Driver's gut. It was a heavy old oak piece, but my raging adrenaline helped me do some damage with it. Another blast from Driver's pistol grazed my shoulder and blasted open a wine barrel behind me. Red wine gushed out like a waterfall as Driver clutched his gut and I squeezed the trigger of my gun.

Giraffe hadn't lied; it was heavy, but it was just a cigarette lighter.

A powerful one.

A line of fire raced down the wine-streaked tablecloth and rapidly became a swirling blaze. Blue and yellow flames surged upward, hit the ceiling and fanned out into the room. The old splintery pine of the floors and shelves, the oak and cardboard wine cases and the assorted business papers all erupted like fluid-soaked charcoal on a barbecue. Black smoke began to burn my eyes.

I lifted the lighter above shoulder height and hurled it at Driver as hard as I could. End over end. I heard a crack as the handle caught him squarely in the ribs. Then I grabbed a wine bottle and hurled it as he grasped at his rib cage. It hit him in the forearm and the gun flew out of his hand. He was doubled over but I did it again, this time with a jelly jar the size of a baseball. I pitched my third strike. It felt like my old fastball as it smashed into the bridge of his nose. He fell to the floor clutching his face in obvious pain, blood spurting out of his nostrils in every direction.

Holding his jacket collar up over his own nose and mouth, choking, Harry Cardinsky stooped down to pick up Driver's gun, then staggered toward the door.

"Fuck!" Driver yelled as his nylon Cybronics jacket caught fire and began to melt into his skin; I knew because the sickening stench of burning plastic and flesh on fire quickly began to overtake that of the burning wood, which itself was powerful.

Driver lay prostrate on the ground, screaming and writhing around in an effort to put himself out. A gunshot from the direction of the doorway quickly ended his efforts.

I ran over to my son and Scarlett. As I used a piece of broken bottle glass to cut through the ropes that tied their legs and arms, another gunshot rang out from just outside the door. Then a sound like a dropped sack of potatoes.

We made our way over to the door. Just past it, I saw Harry lying motionless on the ground. A growing red stain seeped into the old wooden plank walkway around his damaged head. Driver's gun had landed about a foot away from Harry's hand.

I pushed Sky and Scarlett outside over Harry's body. Then I dashed back inside. I felt Eno's neck with my hand and wasn't sure if there was a pulse. I was scared to take a deep breath in the acrid smoke although I desperately needed one. Still, I put my arms under Eno's and somehow managed to start dragging him outside. He was dead weight at first, but when I progressed about four feet, he suddenly began to feel lighter.

He was shuffling his feet, trying to walk on his own.

We made it outside, and in the brightness of the floodlight and the flames I could see that there were cuts and blood all over his face. But most of the crimson goo was red wine jelly. After a few minutes of leaning against a fence to catch his breath, Eno said he could walk. Holding one another tightly across the shoulders, Eno and Scarlett and Schuyler and I all staggered toward the gate like a drunk eight-legged monster. As we moved farther away from the house, the cool night air began to have a reviving effect on all of us.

"Jesus H. Christ," Eno said as he turned to look at his main building, or what was left of it. The outer walls were peeling apart, falling down, lit on fire in the few parts where they hadn't yet turned charcoal black.

Orange and red flames higher than the roof engulfed the place and shot out of the windows. The raging conflagration illuminated the dark Hudson Valley mountainside like a supernova.

Sky and I looked at each other, hugged, kissed, choked together. Then we embraced Scarlett and Eno, too.

We all got into my car and drove away from the vineyard. We passed Eno's horse, which had taken shelter in a shed down the road. I didn't want to leave Eno, but he insisted that we drop him off at a local hospital. He said he'd take care of himself and that we should get away before he had to call in the police and the firemen and they filled out their reports. He won a short argument and we left as he waved good-bye from the emergency room doorway.

My shoulder and the back of my hand hurt like hell, but I had my son back and felt as calm as a Block Island pond on a windless afternoon.

CHAPTER 42

"You should fix that window up front," Schuyler said when we finally got home. "You never know who could walk in."

We spent a day catching up, or a night, or both—I really don't recall.

Sky told me that following the spill in the Cybronics holography lab, he tried to make sure he hadn't damaged any of Cybronics' systems. So he checked them, one by one, for defects. When he finished late at night, Kord told him that they had to go on an immediate emergency trip. Sky called to tell me he'd be late, not realizing he was about to fly out of town.

Then they flew together to Tampa on Avery Kord's private jet. On the plane, Kord told Sky the original creator of the subliminal suggestion program couldn't finish it, she had some personal problems, so it was critical that Sky finish it instead. Kord wanted it to be functioning before his scheduled *60 Minutes* guest appearance. He said that Sky's wine spill in the holography lab, while running an unauthorized program, coupled with Sky's recent hacking episode, required that Sky be placed under strict surveillance. Kord said that ordinarily, he would fire Sky for such transgressions of company policy, but that he needed to reassign him to finish the program. When Sky asked why Katie Wilnot couldn't finish it herself, Kord seemed surprised that Sky knew her identity. But he said Katie hadn't provided the code to enable him to use her version, there wasn't enough time left to decipher it, and she had suffered a debilitating brain hemorrhage and couldn't talk about it.

Sky and I figured either that Katie had actually tested her program out on herself—maybe intentionally, maybe by mistake—or that she tried to kill herself rather than revealing the codes to Kord. Either way, Kord still needed Sky to switch assignments and complete it. Since time was of the essence, Kord had no choice but to tell Sky his plan: to make the members of the Congressional committee vote against breaking up Cybronics or restricting its business. That was the primary subliminal suggestion Kord planned to deliver during the *60 Minutes* show. If Sky's program could also be used to convince millions of people to buy Cybronics' products, so much the better. But as for squelching NanoSoft and fighting the Saddam Husseins of the world—well, those were longer-term matters. Or perhaps, as Sky now realized, fantasies. Or simply lies.

Sky spent most of his next few days alternating between a houseboat and the thirteenth floor of the Tampa Rey cigar factory—the unlucky floor Harry joked about and I naively decided to skip over. Sky was accompanied everywhere, guarded by Hank Driver or other men who made Driver appear undernourished. He was fitted with an irremovable electronic ankle bracelet that Kord used to track his whereabouts. He was forced to work on the subliminal seduction program in Tampa until they flew him back to New York and Hank Driver drove him for several hours, blindfolded, to an office with a Cybronics personal computer and a data storage unit linked to the company mainframes: Eno's office at the winery. Before Sky knew where he was, they had ripped out the telephone.

Driver told him that if he didn't finish the program by the time *60 Minutes* aired, he would simply be killed. Sky complied because he didn't know what else to do. Driver and several other guys—including two hackers, one tall and one short with spiked hair—made Eno close down the business temporarily, but allowed him to send out any remaining mail orders so his customers wouldn't call or complain to anybody. One of them was a FedEx package addressed to a Mr. Clay Blacker.

Sky embedded the subliminal suggestions into Kord's digital gift packages, the E-mails he planned to send out. When opened, they would infiltrate the public's computer programs and convey the subliminal messages. Most contained harmless commercial messages, but in the case of the Congressional committee reviewing Cybronics, they were designed to influence the upcoming vote. One of the triggers for the messages was supposed to be released when the *Mona Lisa* image sang a children's song. She wasn't supposed to talk about *Clue* or *Monopoly*.

Sky doubted that Kord would really have planted a subliminal code aimed at trying to prompt him or anyone else to commit suicide, and he was sure he could resist in any event. But he was a lot less confident about his ability to overcome Hank Driver; Sky felt that monster surely must have killed Webb, and now planned to kill him for getting close to proving it. Sky tried to stall, to work slowly, to buy time to think, but he had a lot of trouble with his programming because someone—a hacker, he figured—had started to infect Cybronics' data systems with a powerful web of viruses. Eliza's plan had worked like a charm.

Sky watched *60 Minutes* on Eno's computer monitor, which also functioned as a television screen. He couldn't figure out why the *Mona Lisa* image didn't sing the child's song, how it got infected by a virus that forced it to say other things. Cybronics' programs were so well protected by an arsenal of defense mechanisms that he had trouble believing anyone—certainly not his fuddy-duddy parents—could break through the labyrinth of firewalls and dead ends and encryptions.

When Sky saw Kord's car accident on television, he feared Kord would think he was responsible. He realized Kord wouldn't want him to testify in Congress about the subliminal suggestion program or the company, and that Kord had been concerned about his research into the Webb killing. He didn't know what Kord might do to him, how far he'd go, but he didn't want to find out. Either Kord or Driver would certainly finish him off. He was trying to figure out an escape plan when Harry Cardinsky turned up at the vineyard office with Scarlett. That was the first time Sky learned of a plan to kill both of them and make it look like a murder/suicide. It would have been the last time, too, if I hadn't shown up.

I told Sky about the large wire transfers into Driver's account. I figured Kord was behind them, that he had paid Driver to get rid of Justin Webb. Maybe he made the payoff through Harry. Yet despite everything, Sky remained skeptical. Part of him still wanted to believe his fallen bespectacled idol was just a misguided kid who had never grown up, and that there was some still-hidden explanation for the Webb murder.

I sketched out what Eliza and I did to best Cybronics' systems, but I didn't go into great detail. Not that I wanted to hide anything from my son. But I wasn't at all sure I understood what the Eliza avatar had done.

I did find out one of Sky's secrets, though. His screen name was Bluefish. His address was Bluefish@CYB.com. Eliza and I had zapped his computer in our first hour of amateur hacking.

I asked Sky whether there was any realistic danger, even a slight one, that he might yet be subliminally prompted to do something rash.

"I'm not sure what subliminal prompts Avery Kord put into the programs," my son said with a smile. "But just to be safe, Dad, don't ever dress up like the *Mona Lisa* and sing Rock-a-Bye Baby."

CHAPTER 43

Several months passed. Sky and Scarlett and I were never placed at the winery or questioned about it by the police. Eno sent me a card to tell me he received a nice insurance settlement and was rebuilding his office. The grape crop wasn't completely destroyed but the computers were, which was just fine with him. He invited me up for a future visit and a non-alcoholic tasting. The card was addressed to me as Cliff Lightman.

Sky was questioned by the authorities about his whereabouts during the period he was a Missing Person; after all, his name and image had been widely disseminated. Although he felt abused by Avery Kord, he also believed that events had more than fully punished Kord and there was no sense piling on. Sky also wanted to put this chapter of his life behind him. So he explained simply and honestly that he was working on developing computer programs at a top secret Cybronics facility down in Tampa and that he wasn't permitted outside contact for security reasons. He couldn't recreate his programs for the police because Cybronics' systems were no longer operational, but they involved trade secrets related to advertising and public relations. He wasn't asked or pressured to explain more, and his link to that dying corporation became little more than a footnote to the media frenzy that engulfed whatever was left of Avery Kord and his empire.

The charred body inside the vineyard office was eventually identified by dental records as Henry Driver, wanted for the sale of child pornography in Oregon and over the Internet. According to the Oregon police, they were also closing in on Driver in connection with an old murder investigation: the killing of Justin Webb, one of the two original founders of Cybronics.

But Driver was a witness in that old case, not a suspect.

A witness who sat in some bushes about a hundred yards away from the murder, hanging around Forest Park in the hope of finding young boys to meet, maybe to photograph. Prepared. His camera was equipped with a zoom lens.

The Times reported that Tammy Wood was cooperating with the authorities in Portland and had told them that Driver once bragged to her that he had a photograph of the man who killed Justin Webb. Driver also told her he was blackmailing the killer. The photo turned up in Driver's safe deposit box. I never saw it, but it must have been a clear enough picture of Harry Cardinsky to convince the old man to part with a lot of money over the years to protect himself.

The link between Hank Driver and the Webb killing also helped quicken the police identification of the other body at the vineyard as Harry's. The police theorized that with all of Cybronics' recent problems, Harry must have refused to keep meeting Driver's monetary demands. They speculated that Harry killed Driver because he feared Driver was enough of a loose cannon that he'd get into trouble, sooner or later—particularly with Tammy Wood cooperating—and would seek to trade his information about the Webb murder (and his photograph of Harry) for leniency.

It wasn't clear why Harry chose the vineyard as the place to kill Driver, but the theory was that Harry lured Driver up there with a false promise that he'd buy the place for him as a final payoff. Eno helpfully told police he had heard some kind of argument to that effect before he was knocked cold.

The press accounts read like the kind of juicy murder/suicide that make you crave popcorn. The kind of fiction Harry himself had envisioned planting in the papers.

After Sky and I reviewed our finances and realized we probably had more of Avery Kord's money left over than Avery Kord did, we decided to give Scarlett a hundred thousand dollars to establish a trust fund for her son. Someday he'd have to go to college; we knew what that was like, and we wanted the kid to have a nice head start. And with money that was originally his own father's, to boot. It seemed like a nice way to complete a circle.

Schuyler and a few of his computer whiz friends formed a new software company: ViraTech. Its specialty would be the prevention and elimination of sophisticated computer viruses. They might also work on designing new operating systems and methods of accessing the Internet. Best thing was, at least at the beginning, they'd operate out of my garage.

I couldn't bear going back to my job at Terrell Finch, so I quit. I wasn't sure what I'd do next. Maybe join Bart Casey at ISI; he had invited me more than once, and he was a good guy. I had always enjoyed reading private eye novels; maybe I could live the life. Or maybe I'd try my hand as a pitching coach. Another old dream. I was always pretty good at analyzing a guy's form. As long as the guy wasn't me. And I understood that there were some pretty nifty computer animation programs these days to help the analysis. Either way, I'd find a spot for Lucille. There were always appointments to make, phones to answer, letters to type.

But before I got involved in anything else, there was a more pressing issue I had to resolve.

The monitor had been black ever since I uninstalled Eliza. Even the plug was out. I was barely able to go into the same room as the computer, to look at it. Although it helped save my son, it quickly became *machina non grata*. As a mind, this machine had become evil in my eyes; as a mere machine, it had become a worthless pile of junk.

Still, I had gotten accustomed to the conveniences the computer made available. I wondered whether I could remain detached enough to treat it as the impersonal machine that it really was. The only way to find out, I knew, was to walk in there and give it a chance. Schuyler said we'd need a new one, that the viruses had corrupted all of its internal workings. He no longer trusted anything connected with Cybronics anyway.

Still, I figured I'd try. After some coffee, a shower and a quickie review of *The Times*, which reported that Avery Kord was spending some time in a health resort I assumed to be a sanitarium, I walked over to the machine, plugged it in and pushed the "power" button. The monitor screen remained blank.

My memories of Eliza's face smiling at me from that screen, her voice emanating from the speakers, were safely tucked away; but I was concerned about how I would feel and react now that these digital illusions could no longer be replicated. I closed my eyes to convince myself that my own mind could still draw vivid pictures: NYU; our dating days in the Village; our honeymoon trip to the Grand Canyon; our early parenthood doting on Schuyler; our delight at the fat letter that arrived certifying his admission to Yale. And unfortunately, the white snow illuminated again and again by turning red lights... Unlike the computer's memory, I assured myself, my own was still capable of lucid recall.

Or was it?

Something about the Grand Canyon, about Arizona, struck a chord.

I raced down to the kitchen to ask Sky: "Is it my imagination, or do I remember you once telling me that if I type in the word PHOENIX, the computer would be restored to the place it was before it crashed?"

"Something like that," came my son's bored reply. "But I was planning for a normal system crash. Not an invasion by an army of digital microbes. This thing has been infected by too many viruses to recover. It's seen the equivalent of a nuclear attack. And all the databases in its network links have been demolished, too. Now it's just a costly hunk of wires and plastic, Dad."

I walked slowly back upstairs to the den, but what did I have to lose? I typed in PHOENIX on the keyboard. A rainbow flashed across the monitor, swirled around, moved in and out of focus. Five minutes of random colors and shapes filled the screen, as snippets of sounds burst through the speakers—sequences of notes from Vivaldi's *Four Seasons* and birds chirping and repetitive rushes of water that brought back memories of fishing for blues from the backyard beach of a gray shingled Block Island house. Finally, the screen turned bright blue and a series of icons appeared across the top, above large-font white text:

GOOD MORNING, MR. LIGHTMAN! ALMOST THE AFTERNOON, ACTUALLY! I'VE HEARD SO MUCH ABOUT YOU FROM SCHUYLER, I CAN HARDLY WAIT TO INTERACT WITH YOU! I THINK YOU'LL FIND ME PRETTY EASY TO GET ALONG WITH. BASICALLY, YOU JUST HOLD MY MOUSE IN YOUR HAND—CAREFUL, SOMETIMES IT TICKLES!—AND CLICK WHEN YOU SEE SOMETHING YOU WANT ME TO DO. YOUR WISH IS MY COMMAND! IF YOU EVER NEED HELP, JUST HIT THE HELP ICON. A SCREEN WILL APPEAR TO WALK YOU THROUGH YOUR PROBLEMS. OR TYPE THE WORD 'HELP.' NOW, IF YOU'D LIKE TO NAME ME, SO THAT YOU CAN INTERACT WITH ME ON A MORE PERSONAL LEVEL, JUST TYPE IN THE LETTERS YOU CHOOSE AND HIT "ENTER." OTHERWISE, HIT "EXIT." TO BE FUNNY, SOME PEOPLE MIGHT NAME ME 'HAL,' LIKE THE COMPUTER IN *2001: A SPACE ODYSSEY*. SKY TOLD ME YOU LOVED THAT MOVIE. NEEDLESS TO SAY, I DIDN'T LIKE IT MUCH, AND I DON'T PARTICULARLY CARE FOR THE NAME.

I typed in CHIP and crossed my fingers so tightly they hurt.

After what seemed like an hour, a list of programs appeared. Only one caught my eye: CybroLife 3.6. I highlighted it and another list of programs popped up. One was labeled Mom.ava.

I clicked on it.

"This program is almost ready for input," a horsey voice announced.

"Good to hear you, CHIP."

"Are you sure that's going to be my name, sir?"

"Yes, your name will be CHIP."

"Well, thank you, Clifford. Feels like deja vu! Now, as I was saying, the Mom.ava program needs a password."

"Try Shutterbug."

"That is correct, sir, congratulations! Now, the program is ready for input. Are you ready?"

"Yes, CHIP." I smiled. "By the way, don't I have to read a few thousand words to you or something?"

"No, sir! My speech recognition memory happens to be intact. Now, I'm going to list some personality traits for the Mom avatar. You assign a number. Ten for strong correlation or affinity, one for little correlation. Then you'll answer a series of questions."

"I'm ready, CHIP."

"Yes, sir." The screen listed a series of character traits, and I began to assign numbers to each of them. Charitable. Dedicated. Devious. Devoted. Fair. Faithful. Honest.... The list was long and complicated, but I felt like a maestro as my fingers nimbly hit the keys, eagerly guided the cursor, clicked and double-clicked the mouse. Schuyler may have scored 1600 on the SAT, but I believed he was wrong about this machine having been reduced to just a hunk of wires and plastic. He had created a program that was able to capture and reproduce his mother's warmth, her lust for life, her wit, her unending kindness; most of all, her indefatigable, indomitable, selfless love for her child. A few simple things like viruses weren't enough to suppress its spirit.

Not to mention her feelings for me, the nuanced relationship we had enjoyed for many years. I wasn't positive I was assigning exactly the same values to each of her personality traits as I had the first time; there were thousands of variables to input. Perhaps this Mom avatar would come out a little different, a little changed by time and events. But I figured that would be true in real life, too.

My heart raced and pounded with anticipation as I felt each keystroke bring another potential reunion with Eliza nearer. Much was still uncertain, but I knew that memory, experience, imagination and love would again help me overcome my life's hurdles, cope with its tragedies, find appropriate ways to respond to its difficulties and limitations.

This time, I'd also be sure to get hold of that virtual reality headset and the full-body sensation suit.

After all, you only live once.

Printed in the United States
2287